never really gone

L.B. ANNE

never really gone

L.B. ANNE

JOA PRESS
FLORIDA

Copyright © 2022 L. B. ANNE. All Rights Reserved. For Information, address JOA Press, P.O. Box 7984. Seminole, FL 33775.
www.joapress.com

Cover creation by May Dawney
Edited by Jessica Renwick
Proofread by Michaela Bush

Library of Congress Control Number: 2022921263

ISBN 978-1-7362688-9-6

To those who love deeply.

never really gone

I can't sleep.

As soon as I close my eyes, I'm back at Micah's funeral. To be honest, I don't even want to try to sleep anymore.

Instead, I look to the right of my bed at Micah's unfinished watercolor mural and remember every bit of the most painful day of my life; the heat in the sanctuary making the perfumes of those around me overpowering, the sniffles and cries, even my own. All of it, so vivid.

I remember thinking, *does it always rain during funerals?* I'd thought that was just a movie cliche to make scenes more forlorn or dramatic, but there was a storm that day. Not while we were tucked inside of Mount Hope Church fanning ourselves. The air

1

conditioning had been out for days, and the sanctuary was so packed with people I was sure we broke the capacity fire code.

I wiped beads of sweat from my forehead. A stream trickled down my neck, disappearing into the ruffled collar of my blouse.

My mother's shoulder pressed into mine. "Are you okay?" she asked.

I pulled the neckline of my shirt away from my sticky skin and rubbed the sweat on my skirt. "Yeah. It's so hot in here."

"It shouldn't be much longer," she said and patted my lap.

The organist's fingers glided over the keys as he played the intro of the next hymn. At least the thrumming of rain would have flooded out Mother Beck's off-key rendition of "His Eye is on the Sparrow."

The wall of stained glass behind her, which usually emanated rays of color, looked dull that day. A choir stood below the massive cross at the center of the wall. They struggled through the hymn. Some members were too overcome to sing, their sweat and tears tinted with makeup and dripping onto their white robes. You had to know Micah to understand. Everyone loved him. He was a magnet for goodness and generosity. When he was around, something good was sure to happen. For instance, a car in front of us paying for our order at the Starbucks drive-thru. Or the time this guy was like, "He kid, here's two tickets to the New York Knicks game tonight. I can't go. You can have them."

At first, I thought things like that happened for no reason at all, but that's not true. It happened to good people, and I benefited because of my proximity to a good person.

How did I get so lucky to have Micah as a boyfriend? Me. With all of my issues. He worked so hard to save me from myself, and now he's the one that's gone. I didn't understand it.

My toes ached from my pointed shoes, and I tugged at the heel, trying to slide my foot out some.

"Stop fidgeting," my mother had whispered. The black veil hanging from her hat grazed my freshly silk-pressed hair, now curling at the roots because of my sweating.

I wished I'd worn a hat with a veil also. And earplugs. And dark glasses.

Watching Micah's mother collapse over his casket in tortured sobs and listening to the wails from those around me had only heightened my emotions.

Many of the mourners lined up to pay their last respects at the casket. Some, still soaked in disbelief, shook their heads and asked, "Why?"

The line moved quickly. My mother joined them, but I didn't. I couldn't move. Soon, I was the only one still sitting on the second-row pew, my eyes lowered, listening.

The body in that casket was not my Micah, and I refused to allow it to become an image embedded in my memory, so I didn't look.

To prepare myself for the funeral, I'd done some research. The part that stuck with me was a rare occurrence, and it was just my luck it would happen. Once a body is placed in a sealed casket, the gases from decomposing can't escape anymore. The pressure increases and the casket becomes like an overblown balloon. It doesn't explode like one, but it can spill out unpleasant fluids and gases. At the thought of it, my stomach twisted, and I grasped it, feeling I might puke.

Breathe, I told myself as I waited for my mother to return and silently prayed Micah wouldn't explode.

Next was the burial. We rode in the limo with Micah's family. His mother insisted on it.

Once we pulled out of the church parking lot, Micah's uncle loosened his tie. "It was a beautiful homegoing service, wasn't it?"

"Yes, it was," my mother replied and squeezed my hand. I was glad she was there to answer because I couldn't. I watched Micah's little brother lean against his mother's bosom and stare at his black patent leather shoes he'd been kicking off the entire day. He didn't make a sound, only looked at his shoes, hardly blinking.

I flipped over the funeral program on my lap. Micah's face smiled up at me from his sophomore year photo as I prepared myself for the worst part of the day—the final goodbye.

The funeral procession led across town to Beacon Cemetery. We entered through a pair of tall white stone pillars and a wrought iron gate, then followed a never-ending road that wound around the burial sections.

We passed beds of chrysanthemums boasting blooms in a kaleidoscope of colors, along with smaller sections of ornamental cabbage plants. I had a passion for flowers and plants. There were few I didn't know. And if I was lucky enough to go to college—meaning, if my family could afford it—I'd become a botanist and own my own nursery one day.

For now, I was satisfied with working part-time at the flower shop around the corner from my house.

The limo came to a stop, followed by more cars than I could count. Six pallbearers—Chase, Micah's older brother, two cousins, and two uncles—carried the casket from the hearse to the grave.

My mother and I followed Micah's family across the lawn to Micah's burial plot.

For a moment, I couldn't breathe. Then my mother's hand grazed my back and she pressed me close to her.

Everyone stood in black suits and dresses around the grave where a mahogany casket covered in an ornate display of white orchids, dahlias, and roses was ready to be lowered into the ground. The smell of fresh cut grass was strong, and it mingled with the scent of Micah's uncle's aftershave beside me.

Chase wore an oversized black raincoat over a black suit. His face was red from crying.

I looked over at him and caught his eye. He gave me a weak smile. I gave him a look that said, I am here. He nodded as if to say, I know.

The sun had shone for a moment when we left Mount Hope Church. But by the time we arrived at the cemetery, the skies were dark and angry. The wind howled. Thunder clapped. Lightning flashed.

It was as if God himself was trying to tell me something.

The funeral director milled around like she was looking for someone, but the lenses of her round glasses were so dark, I was sure she was doing her best not to witness our pain. Maybe she'd known Micah too. By the look of the crowd, the entire city had.

I watched with my head on my mother's shoulder. And just before the casket lowered, I wondered, Is Micah really in there? Maybe all the graves in the cemetery were really empty.

I know. It was an odd thought to have while the minister prayed.

Droplets of rain landed on the casket. One at a time as if someone were dropping them from a single eye dropper. And then, many eye droppers. A torrential downpour.

Black umbrellas popped open here and there, but most didn't seem to mind the weather. It was the least of my worries. Someone sang a hymn, and then a couple of people approached the podium to say a few words. When they finished, the pastor asked for a moment of silence, during which Micah's mother burst into screams. Several people unsuccessfully tried to console her as the casket was lowered into the ground.

I knew exactly how she felt—how each and every person who'd lost someone felt. I knew, because I felt the same way. The same pain. I just had a different way of showing it. There was a dark room inside me that I disappeared into and shut the door. It helped me deal with the numbness and kept me from having to respond to the pain or even eat.

In the end, I was the last person standing at the grave. Soaked and shivering, still looking down at Micah's casket, waiting. But waiting for what?

A lone figure stood several feet away. The only person not dressed in black, he wore a gray hoodie and torn jeans. He waved and walked away.

As I watched the stranger leave, a hand touched my shoulder. "It's time to go, Brie," my mother said, her voice filled with sorrow and pity. She'd gone to get her umbrella from the limo and now held it over me.

I glanced at her, and then down at the grave, then once more at the headstone before I walked away.

In Loving Memory
Micah George
2006-2022

That day, if you had asked me what I thought happened to Micah or anyone after they died, I would've told you I was certain Micah was looking down at us from heaven. That he was shaking his head at us because we took this place a little too seriously. That I'd never see him again.

But today...

I'd tell you we are never really gone.

2

The Night of the Funeral

As far as I was concerned, Micah's death was only true while I was at the funeral. At home, alone, I wouldn't allow myself to believe he was gone. That's when I missed him most and expected him to call or text. I wanted to hear his voice, and one of his stories—even if they were far-fetched—and his always-think-positive attitude which usually annoyed the heck out of me.

I replayed his voicemails just to hear the sound of his voice. It cracked in the older ones and deepened in the more recent. I read his texts to myself frequently and studied the way he'd written the messages. He never used emojis. Ever. So I used as many as I could for him to interpret or just to frustrate him. But Micah loved GIFs, and he used the same ones over and over as if they were the only five or six available in the world. His favorites were of a toddler dancing or pumping his fist in the air and some comedian I didn't know making a face.

I missed Micah so much. I wanted to see him squint at me with annoyance like he did when I had made an argument that made little sense and hear his laugh when my jokes were not funny.

It was two years after the pandemic. We were back in school and happy about seeing each other every day again in person rather than by Zoom, Facetime, Skype, or Meta Portal. We thought we were safe.

No one knew about Micah's heart condition. We found out when he came down with the virus. It happened so fast. One day, he was healthy and laughing his head off into his face mask as I attempted to piggyback him down the hall to the gym. The next thing I knew, he was fighting for his life, unable to breathe without a ventilator.

I never knew if Micah was aware of the hours I sat waiting in the hospital for him to open his eyes. Or if he could feel me holding his hand all those days. I wanted him to see me there and smile. I planned to tell him to get better and that we still had to terrorize Elle and Chase. I wanted to tell him that we had more pranks to pull on our parents and how excited I was about our plans for winter break. Most of all, I wanted to tell him that I loved him— something I'd never been able to say.

But I never got to.

After a few weeks of him being in the hospital, Micah's mother and the school security officer pulled me out of class.

"Micah is awake," she said. "Come with me." Her words, spoken with a slight Caribbean accent, held no sorrow, nor did they hold the happiness I would've expected. She said nothing further and being quiet was not something Mrs. George was known for.

I hurried after her while my mother signed me out at the office. I had no idea that Micah's parents had made the decision—the most difficult choice they had ever had to make. They were transporting Micah to a hospice.

"Okay," I said. Just like that. Like no big deal. I thought it was a rehab center. I'm a teenager, how would I know what a hospice was and that they were taking him there to...

I remember my parents' faces. They had come to console me, I knew. I didn't react right then. Instead, I tried to be strong for Micah's parents. But inside, I screamed. I screamed for Micah not to go.

My mother always says, "You have to stay prayed up, because you never know what may happen, and you won't have the time to ask for forgiveness for your sins." She wasn't a religious fanatic or anything. There were just some things that were non-negotiable. One was her faith. The other was prayer. But her words did cross my mind in those last moments. Had Micah had a chance to pray before his heart gave out? Or did it happen in an instant—gone from breathing on his own without a mask and tube to standing in front of the pearly gates?

The hours after Micah's passing were the most painful time of my life. They turned to days with me barely noticing time passing. I got tired of everyone constantly asking me if I was okay. I wanted to respond with, "Are you? Imagine if you were fifteen and your sixteen-year-old boyfriend died. Would you be okay?" I don't know why people ask when they know you're not. You can be there for someone without asking that or even speaking.

No matter how much I tried to fake it, I wasn't okay. And it wasn't just about losing my best friend. Or that I missed him so much I thought my heart would explode. Something else was happening.

I'd just gotten out of the shower. I grabbed my robe from the hook on the door, slipped into it, and then switched on my blow dryer. The cool air quickly cleared the steam from the mirror. I stood for a long time, staring at my reflection, my long wavy hair dripping over my back. My swollen eyelids. I didn't know what I was looking for. I felt empty. Maybe I was looking for the Gabriella that was strong enough to get through the coming days without Micah.

I sighed, scrunched a towel through my strands, and shook my hair.

That's when I saw him.

Micah's image materialized in the mirror beside mine.

"Micah?" I gasped and dropped the towel. My hand flew up, covering my open mouth.

Wait. Don't cue the ominous music. It wasn't spooky. Micah didn't float in like a ghost or suddenly appear with a flash of light. It was a gentle entrance.

He wasn't smiling, but he looked peaceful. I blinked, then looked away from the mirror and to my right, expecting to find him standing there. But he wasn't. When I returned my gaze to the mirror, his image was gone, replaced by the reflection of my bedroom behind me.

I continued to stare into the mirror, not quite sure what to make of the image I had just seen.

My heart sank. I covered my face with my hands and whined into them with short breaths before resting them on the sink. I stared at the chipped black polish on my fingernails and then back at the mirror at my red eyes, certain I was having some kind of psychotic break. I shook my head and turned away trying to push the image of Micah out of my mind.

I switched off the bathroom light, climbed in bed with my wet hair, and curled into a ball on my side. I prayed and had high hopes that sleep would find me. But I guess God wasn't in the mood to answer prayers. At least not that night.

When it was obvious I wasn't going to sleep, I got out of bed and walked over to my desk. I sat at it and picked up the family-sized bag of peanut M&Ms I'd gotten for Micah. There's a commercial that asks what you would do for whatever ice cream they were advertising. Well, for Micah it was, what would you do for peanut M&Ms. Seriously, he had been addicted to them. I'd planned on giving the bag to him when he recovered. I'd toss one in the air, and he'd catch it in his mouth. That's what we always did until he almost choked one day. Two minutes later, he was laughing and eating them like nothing had ever happened.

I picked up my phone and swiped through the photos. Cute ones of when Micah went out to eat with my family. He and my dad standing together. Micah smiling and posing while my dad had a crooked grin and looked stressed as usual. Many of our memories were from school. Football games, dances, hanging out after class. I tried not to cry, but the thought of being at Lincoln High without Micah seemed too much to bear.

The days and nights between the funeral and the day I went back to school blurred together. My parents said it was time to get back to the world of the living. What? Had I been a vampire or something—vacationing in the world of the dead? Okay, Micah had been right. My jokes weren't funny.

I felt numb walking into Lincoln High. Everything seemed blah, like a movie that had gone from color to black and white. Or maybe food with no flavor. Yeah, that was a better analogy. I expected everyone to be weird. We were all mourning. Micah's best friend met me with a hug. A hug that meant everything. It said, *I understand your never-ending pain.*

We were equally surprised to see each other back at school so soon. I could tell he'd been crying. Just being there, in our hall, without Micah felt off. It was going to take a while to get used to.

"Come on, Chase. Stop it," I said, wiping away a tear that rolled down his cheek and over the peach fuzz he called a mustache. He and Micah had always joked they'd be shaving soon. "I know," I said. "Being here without him is hard."

Chase sniffed and ran his hand over his short dreadlocks. "He was like the heartbeat of this place, wasn't he? Maybe it was too soon to come back."

"I don't believe there's ever a right time." It was a fact. Even if we would have come back a year later,

Micah still wouldn't have been here, and being at school would have felt just as awkward.

Chase opened his jacket, revealing a button pinned on the inside with Micah's yearbook photo.

I touched it gently. "Gone, but never forgotten? Whose idea was that?"

"I don't know, but the whole school got them."

"That's so very 80s of them."

"Don't worry, I grabbed you one." Chase leaned against the locker behind him. "Did you see the display case on the way in?"

"The memorial of all the students we lost to the virus? Yes. I didn't know there were twelve."

"I don't think I can take it happening again. Even if I don't know them. Maybe I should see if my parents can have me transferred to a new school."

I opened my locker and lifted my books from the shelf. "And leave me here?"

"You can come with," he said with a grin.

"I was about to say," I quipped.

Chase cleared his throat. "I know this all just happened, but I cannot get used to not seeing Micah running up the hall, late for class." He held his hand toward the side entrance. "I mean, like right now, he should be coming through those doors." Chase shook his head. "He always ran late, didn't he? And when I picked him up, he made us both late."

"Yeah," I said, trying not to picture it. Micah had always been late because it had been his job to get his younger siblings off to school. His mother worked crazy hours. At that time in the morning, she would have either already left for work or just gone to sleep after a night shift. And he never complained about it—not once.

A few other students joined us, all wearing Micah's button. Most expressed similar sentiments. Everyone missed Micah and expected things to be different. I listened and offered support.

That was just how I was. No matter how much I was screaming inside, I kept my feelings hidden behind that door, while I did my best to encourage others.

Chase walked me to class and continued on to his own, a head taller than everyone else in the hall— even with his shoulders slumped and hands in his pockets.

As I entered, a boy rushed up and knocked into me as he went inside. I stumbled and almost dropped my books. He glanced over his shoulder. "Oh, sorry, Brie."

I ignored him and looked around for a place to sit. *I can do this. Take it day by day,* I told myself. Shannon's twenty-braceleted arm shot up when she saw me. She patted the chair beside her, and I went and plopped down into it.

"Thanks for saving me a seat," I said.

She pulled her braids out of the back of her jacket. "Of course. I've been doing it every day until the bell rings. I'm glad you're back. None of these heifers will let me copy their work," she joked. "So how are you? Are you okay?"

"I'm managing," I replied as I took out a notebook and a pen.

"Me too. He was a good guy. I'm going to miss him."

It was kind of Shannon, but at the same time I thought, *OMG! How many friggin' times am I going to have to hear "are you okay" today?* The words were my new pet peeve. I decided the next person who asked me was getting shot in the face with a rubber band.

"Here." Shannon passed me a slip of paper.

"What is this?" At a quick glance, it looked like Monopoly money.

"A gift certificate from me. People don't know what to say when someone dies. Some can be downright rude. That certificate entitles you to five slaps. Whoever you point at, I'll commence to slapping."

Usually, I would've howled with laughter at her antics. There was no doubt in my mind Shannon would do it. Instead, I smiled and acted like I was paying attention to the teacher.

For the next few days, I sat through my classes, listening to the hum. That's what I called the voices of my teachers and classmates. I didn't understand anything they said. I heard hum of their tones intermingling, while I thought about other things. I think my teachers could tell I was somewhere else, but they didn't say anything or call on me to answer questions. One even caught me staring out the window and only smiled. A smile that said, *It's okay, you get a pass today.*

Each day at lunch, I forced myself to drink something. Eating was still out of the question. But that wasn't the hardest part of lunch period. The hardest part was leaving. So many memories took place outside of those double doors.

Micah's locker was at the end of the hall. Sometimes he shared mine, or I used his. I passed by the wall of windows that allowed you to see inside the cafeteria, hoping no one watched me having a flashback meltdown. *Don't do it, Gabriella. Don't you let them see you break.*

I choked back the tears, picked up my pace, and took a big breath, remembering an afternoon in that hallway when Micah had grazed my arm with his. I'd looked up at him. And when his eyes met mine, I'd felt something that I can only describe as divine. Peace and love, comfort and assurance. Micah had taken my hand and stopped me in my tracks. I remembered how he grinned—not a full grin, but just enough. His grasp was always gentle, and his hand warm and strong. His touch made me feel secure and safe. He had to have known I loved him. *Why didn't I tell him?*

I gave myself a moment to breathe deeply and collect myself before continuing to class. My head drooped as I walked, and I barely noticed the hum of students around me.

Before long, the last bell rang, and I was released from the prison of trying to act *normal*. But only for a few minutes, before I'd need to do another *normal* performance for my parents to keep them from worrying about my mental state.

I walked outside past a group of students who stopped talking when they saw me and into the throng of kids waiting at the crosswalk. The crossing guard blew his whistle, and we plodded across the street to the grocery store parking lot.

The school lot was so crowded that it was easier for my mother to pick me up over there. She smiled and waved as I approached her blue Tuscon. Then, acting as if the windshield were tinted dark enough for no one to notice, my mother leaned on the steering wheel, tilted her head, tucked her lips, and looked up her nostrils in the rear-view mirror. I normally would have tried to restrain my amusement; my mother was never embarrassed about doing those sorts of things in public, even pulling her pants out of her crack. Embarrassment was not a part of her DNA. Or was it discretion that wasn't? But as far as I was concerned, humor didn't exist anymore.

I opened the front passenger door, slid into the seat, and turned the air vent away from my face. My mother greeted me with her usual, "Hey, Brie-Brie. How was your day?" and some other stuff I barely heard.

"It was fine."

"Just fine?"

"Yep." I chewed on my bottom lip and shifted my backpack on the floor between my feet. A flash reflected in the side mirror. I almost gasped when I turned to it. Micah's dark brown eyes watched me. He looked exactly as he had that last time I'd seen him healthy, with his hair freshly cut and his face smooth. But there was something different about him now. He stared at me intensely before he faded into a reflection of the parking lot behind us: a shopping cart rolling by and a row of cars with kids climbing in.

"Brie, are you okay?" asked my mother.

I groaned internally. But no, I did not shoot my mother in the face with a rubber band. At that moment, I didn't even remember I'd said I would do that.

"Yes, I-I…" I couldn't find words, so I just stopped talking, stumped. *I'm losing it.*

We drove in silence, and my mother glanced at me every couple of minutes. My hand rested on the center console between us. At times, my mother grabbed my hand and gave it a light reassuring squeeze. Other times, she rubbed it.

When we got home, she dropped me off in front of the house. I hurried inside, up the stairs, and straight to my room. I threw my backpack and jacket on the bed, then paced the floor, clenching and unclenching my fists.

I stood in front of the mural behind my bed for a moment, staring at Micah's unfinished artwork. A portion of the wall was purple—my favorite color—and an array of flowers angled down from the ceiling and across the wall. The rest of the wall was white with only an outline of flowers.

I turned and faced the bathroom.

Okay. I shook my hands as if I were shaking water off and walked inside. I stood in the dark, staring at the mirror. *What are you waiting for?* I inched my hand toward the light switch. When I flicked it on, I wanted Micah to be there. At the same time, I didn't.

Just as I was about to flip the light on, my phone chimed and played "Always Be My Baby."

I gasped. It was the ringtone I used for Micah's calls only.

"Is that you?" I said aloud. "Micah?"

I shook my head and almost laughed. I didn't believe in that stuff. I pulled out my phone, almost expecting the text to be from him.

It was.

Gabby, I am not where I'm supposed to be.

I couldn't believe it. Right there on my phone—Micah!

I dropped the phone onto my bed and backed away, covering my mouth with my hands.

It couldn't be Micah. It just couldn't. My family were Christians and accustomed to how things worked with life and death, heaven and hell. We understood that when a person died, they went somewhere else. Hopefully, somewhere better. God called them home. At least, that's what we believed. A wake is held for loved ones to view the body and give them a chance to see the person one last time.

And people bring hams and cakes to the family's home. The next day is the funeral, and that's the end of it.

So how was it possible that I saw Micah and received a text message from him? It went against everything I thought I knew. How could it be him? But Micah was the only person who called me Gabby. Everyone else called me Brie, short for Gabriella.

Wait, everyone knows Micah called me Gabby. Why would someone do this to me? My stomach clenched. *I'm not playing this game. Ugh, I can't stand people sometimes.*

My fingers flew across the keypad as I replied:

This is a cruel joke. How did you get his phone? Trust me, I will find out who you are, and when I get through with you, you're going to wish you still had fingers to text with.

I tapped send and huffed. *There. Respond to that, phone thief! Oh my gosh, did I just threaten to cut someone's fingers off? Whatever.*

I paced my room and kicked the giant pink stuffed pig my dad had won for me at the summer carnival a few years before, waiting for a response. It never came.

"Hmph." I looked for the name or phone number the message came from. But there was none. Not even Micah's name. Only 01001000 01100101 01100001 01110110 01100101 01101110 in a continuous string.

What is that? I'm in the Matrix. I pinched my arm. I scratched my hand. "Ouch," I said. Yep, I was awake.

I tossed my phone on the bed, placed one hand on my hip, and rubbed my forehead with the other. *This is crazy. I'm acting crazy. But what if it was Micah? I just threatened him. No, it wasn't him. This stuff doesn't happen. Wouldn't someone have mentioned it at church or something? Or one of those pastors on television?*

I think a teen like me—who tried to pay attention in church because her mother expected her to answer questions about the sermon later—would have remembered someone saying, "After you die, God will allow you to stick around for a while, appear in mirrors, and send texts."

My phone dinged with a call, jarring my thoughts. I stared at it resting on my unmade bed. Instead of picking it up, I backed away, bumping into the window, and waited, shifting my weight from one foot to the other. I was afraid. Afraid it could really be Micah, yet also afraid it wasn't. *This is like a horror movie*. Next, I would find out someone was in my house, trying to kill me. I went to my closet and dug out my old softball bat from the corner behind the boxes of notebooks, pictures, and everything I'd created since first grade, just in case.

The phone wouldn't stop dinging. *A normal person would've hung up already*. Finally, I picked it up and looked at the notification: Dad Calling.

"Hello?"

"Brie? Are you alright?"

I shot an invisible rubber band at the phone. "Dad? Yes, why?"

"You didn't pick up. I've been calling—"

"Uh, yeah, I fell asleep." I let out a loud, fake yawn.

"Oh, okay... You actually slept?"

"Why did you say it like that?" I sat on my bed. *Do they know I'm up all night?*

"Honey, we check on you. We can see you're awake."

Great. Whatever happened to privacy?

"Plus," my dad continued, "you have dark circles and bags under your eyes. You *look* like you're not sleeping."

"Well, I'm fine, Dad. No need to worry."

"Sorry, kid, but I'll worry until you're eighty. Gotta get back to work. I'll see you later. And Brie…"

"Yes?"

"It's going to be okay. Really. We understand what you're going through. We miss him too. Micah will always live in your heart."

The call disconnected.

I held the phone to my chest. "In my heart is not what I'm concerned about."

That night, I sat on the edge of my bed and stared out the window. A full moon lit up the dark sky. I remember reading that a piece of the moon broke off. That's about what my heart felt like.

The person playing the prank with Micah's phone never responded, and I decided it was just that—a prank.

I laid down and pulled the covers over my head so my parents wouldn't see me cry if they checked on me. All I could think about was why I'd never told Micah that I loved him and how I'd never had those feelings for anyone before. What would've happened if I had told him? Love was a strong word that I'd reserved only for family. I'd witnessed how it could cause as much pain as joy, so I'd never wanted to use it lightly. My parents loved each other, but they argued a lot. They thought that because their discussions usually took place in their bedroom, we couldn't hear them yelling or my mother shedding tears.

If that was love, I didn't want it.

Micah had changed that. He had been my first real boyfriend other than Tony. But I was only five years old when I "dated" Tony. And I'd punched him in the stomach, chased him around the playground monkey bars, and told him he was my boyfriend. Sure, I'd had a few crushes along the way. But that's where I'd left them—in the crush zone.

With Micah, I had become so comfortable with him as my best friend, I hadn't wanted him to think I'd liked him more than he'd liked me. Which, in case you're wondering, was a lot.

Micah had shared his feelings first. One afternoon, he'd sat at the glass coffee table in our family room with tiny bottles of acrylic paint. Holding one of my Chucks close to his face, he painted the same flowers he'd eventually paint on my wall. I'd been lounging on the couch, watching him work.

"Do you think we should officially date?" he had asked without looking up. "If you don't think it's too weird." His brush stopped moving. "I mean, exclusively."

I hadn't known what to say. "Uh…"

"I'll take that as a yes." Micah gave me that knowing smirk that drove me nuts (in a good way).

Our relationship starting like that saved me from going through the whole *oh-my-gosh-he-looked-at-me/sweaty-armpit* phase, which had been a relief.

I don't know why, but us dating had made sense. I mean, we'd already known so much about each other. And we were always together, talking or texting about something. The last time I'd played wingman for him at the coffee shop, I'm sure he'd noticed that I'd gotten a little jealous when he flirted with that girl from our rival school. I'd been shocked too.

It wasn't long before one night at the movies, he'd said those three words. No, not "More popcorn please." He'd told me he loved me. He'd whispered it and then taken a sip of his drink. "I love you, Gabby," he'd said without fear or trepidation. In turn, I had stuffed my face with popcorn until my cheeks ballooned. Then suddenly, I'd choked on a kernel, and Micah performed the Heimlich maneuver on me to dislodge it. Sheesh, who does that? They'd stopped the film and everything.

Now, footsteps creaked on the stairs, pulling me from my memories. My parents were on the way. Night patrol. I pushed the covers off my head and breathed slowly and deeply. I could sense them in the doorway, looking in on me. I kept my eyes shut, and moments later, heard them walk away. My performance was a success.

I could probably count on both hands the number of times I prayed as a teen, other than when Micah was sick. And I mean on my own—by my own volition—and not the *now-I-lay-me-down-to-sleep* kind of prayer. That night probably took me into double digits.

I folded my hands in front of me. "Please give me a sign. If Micah contacting me is real, let me know and help me deal with it. Show me what I'm supposed to do. But if this is the work of the devil, cast it into the pit of hell. Amen."

I was exhausted, but sleep would not come. I tossed and turned for a few minutes, then my phone lit up on my nightstand. I grabbed it and looked at the notification.

You have a friend request from Shaun Murphy.

Shaun Murphy? Why did that name seem familiar? *From school?* My thoughts were muddled because of the lack of sleep and all I was going through, but I didn't do stupid things. I didn't press confirm. There were too many predators on social media. I tossed my phone aside, and hours later, watched the sun light up my yellow curtains.

I showered in the dark that morning and didn't know what I looked like when I left for school. That was not an abnormal occurrence. Many people didn't have mirrors in the 1800s, but it was the year 2022, so maybe that wasn't a good argument.

If I wore makeup, not using a mirror may have been a problem. But I didn't wear makeup, so it wasn't. I could easily use my acne treatment pad and face moisturizer in the dark. All I had to do was reach up and run my fingers across my cheeks and forehead. And I could put on my tinted lip balm without looking in a mirror.

Next, I pulled a headband over my hair and let it hang around my neck. I didn't need to look to brush my locks into a high ponytail and pull the headband over my hairline.

So that was the plan—to avoid mirrors as much as possible while trying to figure out how to stop my mind from manifesting Micah. And to not tell anyone, because I'd already spent three years in therapy for other reasons. I was doing well, considering. I made sure I stuck to my treatment plan and had stopped weighing myself.

My plan worked for the first half of the day, but the next thing I knew, I left the media center and heard Micah's voice. "Gabby!"

I froze. *Micah?*

4

This is not happening.

I'd seen Micah, received a text, and now heard his voice loud and clear, like he was really at school with me? I didn't want to turn around and have people see me react to this ghost in my head. So I started walking again. Maybe I could outrun the figment of my imagination.

Morgan appeared in the crowd of students and rushed over to me. "Whoa, Brie." She put her hand on my arm to stop me and pointed a long square fingernail behind us. "Officer Spencer is calling you."

"Oh, really? I have my earbuds in. I didn't hear him."

Morgan looked at me oddly over her glasses. Clearly, she could see I didn't have earbuds in because of my ponytail.

I tugged at my earlobe. "Uh, ha-ha... That was a joke."

Officer Spencer walked over to us and nodded at me. "Hey, Gabby."

I'd forgotten he'd been calling me that ever since he'd heard Micah say it.

"I'll see you later." Morgan spun on her heel and took off toward the stairs.

Officer Spencer wasn't your normal school security officer. He actually talked to us. I mean, not like how most adults talk to children. What we had to say meant something to him. You could always find him near one of the exit doors or any of the regular school hiding places for doing things you weren't supposed to, like using your phone, skipping class, or making out in a dark corner. How do I know that? I plead the fifth.

There was a rumor that his son had died a couple of years ago because some stupid kid was playing with a gun. I didn't know if it was true. That's not something you just ask someone because you're curious.

Many of my classmates had crushes on him. Anyone could see it. They'd start wearing makeup and walking past him a lot. And he usually responded with, "Go wash your face. You're a child wearing too much makeup. It's unbecoming. Do your parents know you're wearing that? Maybe I should give them a call." I'd seen him fake those calls in front of the girls. Surprisingly, the girls returned to school the next day without their false eyelashes and overly glossed lips.

Micah always went to him when he'd had questions about anything—life, people, sports. Officer Spencer was always helpful.

Now, he gave me a kind smile. "I'm not going to ask if you're doing okay, because I know you're not. I wouldn't be."

Finally, someone understands. I didn't have to shoot him in the face with a rubber band. I could see myself running through the hall, dodging students, and this muscle-bound policeman with skinny legs chasing me down and tackling me.

For a moment, Officer Spencer's eyes looked misty, and then they cleared. "I'm praying for you and Chase and Micah's family. If you need anything, my wife and I are here for you."

"Thank you," I replied.

His shoulders stiffened as he shifted into officer mode. "Hurry and get to class. Don't let me catch you wandering the halls after the bell rings." He shot me a quirky grin, and I smiled back.

It was a lighter day. I still heard the hum of everyone around me, and I still felt like I was walking through a dream, but it didn't seem as heavy as it had before. And for once, there were no signs of Micah. I believed my mental state was improving.

Until later that night.

I reached for the handle of our stainless-steel refrigerator to grab my dad some ice for his drink. Micah's blurry reflection on the fridge door caught me off-guard. It looked like he stood behind me! I froze, not sure what to do.

"Brie? Are you getting the ice?" asked my father, barely glancing up from his meal. My mother sat next to him, cutting her chicken. My sister was in her usual seat across from them, stabbing a fork into her mac and cheese.

My mind whirled as I pulled the door open and grabbed a package from the freezer. "Uh huh."

"Excuse me? The ice?"

"Oh, yeah, I've got it." I went to the table and handed it to him, then returned to the refrigerator.

There was only my blurry reflection on the door now.

When I turned back to my father, he stood behind me, holding out a package of frozen spinach.

"I don't want that. Why are you giving me spinach?" I asked.

He frowned. "I asked for ice. This is what I got."

"I didn't give you that."

"Yes, you did," said my mother.

My parents stared at me. My dad's face began to turn red, and that wasn't good.

My little sister nodded, looking up from her plate. "You did. You're acting weird."

"Shh," my mother told her.

I took the spinach and set it on the counter. "Oh, sorry," I said. "A lot on my mind. School. Assignments and stuff. I'll get your ice."

"No, I'll get it. You sit down." He took his phone from his pocket and dialed a number.

"What are you doing?" I asked. "You never allow us to use our phones during dinner."

"Put the phone down, Lorenzo," said my mother. "Just wait. Let's all sit down and have a nice supper."

He gave her a disgruntled look, then shoved his phone into his pocket. Something was up with them. I felt a speech coming. I sat at the table as my mother watched me. My mother was always beautiful. Happy or mad, you couldn't deny it. Flawless ebony skin and arched full brows and that one dimple. But fine lines were making a permanent place on her forehead.

"Brie," my mom started. "I think it's time we have you talk with someone."

I crossed my arms. "Nope. Not interested. We're already in family therapy."

"No, I mean about grieving," she said. "Just once, and then you can decide if you want to continue. You hardly sleep. You're not eating … "

I took the serving spoon and placed a scoop of mac and cheese on my plate. Then I took some candied yams and even a spoonful of string beans.

They waited—even my little sister—until I took a bite of the macaroni. As I chewed, I could feel the pressure releasing from the room like the air from a balloon that hadn't been tied at the end. Everyone relaxed.

"She's eating, she's eating," my little sister sang.

My mother smiled at me.

"Trying to," I replied, slowly chewing. I ate a couple more bites and set my fork down. My stomach wasn't happy. It kept pinching, as if to say,

"You can't go without eating, and then hit your digestive system with mac and cheese!"

My mother must have thought making my favorite meal would get me to eat. It worked for three bites—one of mac and cheese and two of candied yams.

She gave me a concerned look. "Honey, you have to eat more than that."

I rubbed my stomach. "I know. I'm really trying, but my stomach…"

My father's chair squeaked as he pushed away from the table. I braced for him to go off. Any minute, he'd go from English to Italian with his lecture. But he didn't. He pulled his wallet from his pocket and removed a crisp fifty-dollar bill. He set it between me and my mother's plates and looked at me.

"Eat, and it's yours."

My sister's eyes widened. "No fair!"

He raised a brow at me. "What do you say?"

Bribery, really? Will bribery take away the pain in my heart or the sunken feeling in my chest or the fog I'm walking through every day? Will it make me hear properly again, instead of just the hum of voices?

He tapped the bill. "Think about it."

My parents finished their meals and rose from the table. My sister stayed behind and sulked as she watched me push a tiny piece of garlic over a string bean.

After my parents rinsed their plates and left the room, she leaned close to me. "Brie," she whispered. "Give me half the money, and I'll eat it for you."

Elle drove me nuts, but she was my mini-me, and I loved her to pieces. I'd never admit that to her face though. As I liked to say, "There was no Ella without Gabriella." That's where her name came from. We called her Elle for short. We were as close as sisters could be and were six years apart. The "divorce baby" was what I had heard someone call her when she was born.

My parents had been at a rough patch in their marriage and separated for a while. The gossipers who were supposed to be my mother's friends at the time said she got preggers to keep my father. It's crazy how kids know gossip. I'd heard everything.

At the time, I thought I was the reason he'd left. That I wasn't good enough. Because I was, you know, a bit heavier than other kids. To tell the truth, I was a lot heavier. Whatever the reason, my parents got back together, but something was definitely off. My father became moody and distant and spent more time away from home, at the office, or in the downtown bars. Yep, I heard about that too. But after Elle was born, it was like I had my dad back again. So she wasn't the divorce baby, but the family-saving baby.

Elle's eyes danced with excitement. She clearly hoped that I would take her up on her offer.

"Yes," I whispered, not because I wanted her to eat for me. I wanted her to have the money.

Elle did a soft clap and hopped on her seat. She pointed at me. "But first, you have to eat one more bite of everything."

"You've got a deal."

"Promise?"

I nodded.

"Cross your heart and hope to—I mean, okay." She took my plate and scraped off her portion, leaving a few bites for me.

At last, I had food in my belly, and it was a welcomed relief. It made it easier to sleep. I finally drifted off, laying on my side with storm sounds playing from my phone—rain pattering against a tin roof with a gentle crack of thunder every now and then.

I dreamed of Micah that night. The storm sound probably brought it on. I stood over his grave in the cemetery. The rain came down hard, and the thunder and lightning seemed to be right overhead. I heard a voice behind me and turned to see his figure standing between gravestones, enveloped in fog.

The fog cleared as I approached Micah. He watched me and lifted his hand. I lifted mine. They came together but didn't touch—stopped by an invisible wall.

"Stay," I said.

Micah merely looked at me as he backed away.

"Why can't you stay?" I cried.

Then he was gone. And I was alone, crying out to him, as a soft mist rolled across the graves. I threw my head back and screamed at the overcast sky. Releasing all the anger inside me.

I awoke mid-scream with my mother's arms around me. "It was just a dream," she repeated into my hair as she rocked me.

I held onto her as if I would drop off a cliff if I let go, remembering what I heard as I awoke.

"I'm still here, Gabby."

5

Those four words were on my lips when I awoke the second time. "I'm still here, Gabby."

My mother was gone. She probably left after she was sure I was sound asleep. My phone blinked a couple of times, then went dark. It was six a.m. Outside my window, the sky was starting to turn from a deep, dark blue to a lighter gray-blue. I climbed out of bed and groggily stumbled to the bathroom. I flipped on the light switch, immediately remembering I shouldn't.

A handprint stood out starkly on the mirror.

A whole handprint, as if someone had taken a hot shower and placed their hand on a steamed mirror. The shower was dry. The room was dry. I lifted my hand above it. It was larger than mine. The print slowly disappeared.

"I'm still here, Gabby," Micah's voice said inside my head.

I went from not seeing Micah at all to seeing his reflection everywhere. Storefront windows, the doors of cars. He always wore the same expression.

"No, no, no, no," I whispered every time I saw it, as if that could stop me from going nuts. I would glance at it, and then at the ground as I power-walked away.

At school one day, I kept my head down as I hurried through the hall, turning the ringer off on my phone. I missed a step and bumped into someone in front of me. He reached to steady me, but I pulled away. I apologized and mumbled something about being clumsy. As I spoke, I looked up and saw my reflection in the media center glass doors. And faintly, Micah.

I hurried to class, and Chase bounded the steps after me. "Brie, I've been looking all over for you. Why haven't you been taking my calls?"

I walked backward until he caught up to me, hoping I didn't still look freaked out. "When have you called?"

"Constantly," he replied. "I need to talk to you."

I stopped, held the straps of my backpack, and looked around. "Am I not right here in front of you? Talk."

Chase grabbed my elbow and pulled me to the side. "No, not here."

"Dude, why do you look so frumpy? Either tuck in your shirt or pull it out. You can't have it both ways. And fix your collar." I pulled his collar from inside his shirt.

Chase shoved my hand away. "Right now, I don't care about any of that."

"Why not? What's going on? Is it a girl? You can't fight a girl. Do you want me to jack her up? You know I'll do it," I joked, thinking it would calm him.

"No, Gabby, listen," he said seriously. "I cleared out Micah's locker for his parents. And..."

I sighed. "What?"

"There's something I need to show you. I found something interesting."

"Something like what? Give it to his parents."

"I can't. You have to see it." Chase's eyes pleaded with me.

"Okay. After school. Umm... the coffee shop in the plaza across the street."

"Good. Good. We're doing this," he said, hitting his fist into his hand and twisting it. "I'll see you. And turn your phone on."

He took off to class without even a wave.

I tried to stay calm as I walked to the coffee shop. *What could be so important about whatever was in Micah's locker?* Then it hit me. A love note. Micah had been seeing someone else, and Chase didn't know how to tell me. A lot of girls had liked Micah. But wouldn't Chase have already known about something like that? They were best friends.

Ashlyn ran toward me as I stepped onto the sidewalk. "Brie!"

"Uh, hey," I replied.

Before I could walk away, she hugged me. I planted my arms to my sides and didn't return the embrace. I barely knew her. In fact, I didn't think she liked me much from the little interaction we'd had. She rarely spoke to me in class. Only the occasional, "Do you have a pen?" or "Psst! Pass this note."

And there was that time in junior high school when she'd called me "Chunkified." Everyone had laughed. I'd wanted to beat the crap out of her.

Slowly, I'd stood from my desk and turned toward her.

"Look, she's getting up," her friend told her.

"So what are you going to do?" Ashlyn said as she stood.

I put my hands on my hips. Her question triggered a strong desire in me to punch her face in.

"Girls!" said the teacher.

Ashlyn's smile turned into a frown.

I pointed at her. "What did you call me?"

"Nothing."

"No, you called me something. What?" I stepped in front of her.

"No, I didn't." She stepped back and bumped into the desk behind her.

My hands squeezed into fists as I stepped closer to her.

She glowered at me. "Okay, I called you 'Chunkified.'"

"Chunkified?" I repeated.

Ashlyn had chuckled nervously. "Yeah."

I grabbed her by the neck and pushed her against the wall. "I will snap your neck."

She couldn't have weighed a hundred pounds. I was a good buck-eighty. Boy, if the teacher hadn't intervened... Anyway, back then, I would fight at the drop of a hat.

Ashlyn never called me a name again, nor did anyone else at that school. At least, not to my knowledge. Plus, by freshman year, I'd gotten down to a size ten.

That's why it was so shocking that she hugged me.

"I, uh..." Ashlyn pushed her auburn waves of hair from her face.

"Ashlyn, it's okay. Really." There was no need for her to go through the whole *I'm-sorry-about-Micah* and *I'm-sorry-you're-going-through-this* speech.

She shook her head and then nodded. "It's just that...my boyfriend..." She paused, biting her lip. "I understand what you're going through. Okay? He's gone—who knows where—and I don't know— I just..."

She broke into sobs and jogged away.

"Ashlyn!" I watched her back as she threw her hands down. She ran faster, then turned the street corner and disappeared from view.

What was that? I stood there stunned for a moment and then hurried to the coffee shop.

A bell chimed when I pushed open the door, and Chase looked up from his table next to the side window. The smell of freshly ground coffee beans and chocolate was a welcomed distraction from my thoughts.

The coffee bar took up the back of the shop, and there were four tables each with two chairs, beside the windows and along the wood-planked wall. Four people stood in line at the cashier, waiting to place an order.

I approached Chase's table, and he looked out the window at the busy street.

"Hey." I slid into the seat across from him and glanced at the black cement ceiling and ducts. I took off my jacket and hung it over the back of my chair.

"Hey," he replied. "What was that outside with Ashlyn?"

I shrugged. "You know, I just asked myself the same thing. When I have an answer, I'll share it with you."

"Don't bother. Let Ashlyn's business stay Ashlyn's business. I have enough on my mind already." He gestured at the sign behind the coffee bar. "You want something? Coffee, tea, croissant?"

"Such a gentleman. No, thanks."

"If you're sure."

"Yeah. Tell me. What's up?"

Chase held his coffee cup with both hands. "Remember that time you fell doing your routine on the football field?" He laughed. "You just laid there, too embarrassed to get up. Why did you lay there?" he asked. "Did you think you were invisible? Micah ran out and helped you up, then did the routine with you. Remember that? Man, he could dance, right?"

My heart panged at the memory. "Dang, why you gotta be that guy?"

He tilted his head. "What guy?"

"The one who brings up all your embarrassing moments."

Chase smirked. "Micah was a good guy though. Remember that."

Why wouldn't I remember it? That was odd.

Chase let go of his coffee cup, leaned forward, and wrapped his warm fingers around mine.

I gave him a sideways look. "Okay, what's going on? You're freaking me out."

"I found something," he said.

"I know. You said that already. What?"

Chase glanced around the coffee shop, making sure nobody was listening to us, and lowered his voice. "Micah was involved in something."

"Something *you* didn't know about?" I asked. "That doesn't sound right. He told you everything."

"I'm not sure we knew him as well as we thought. I found a note." His eyes searched mine, then he slid a crumpled paper across the table.

I stared at it. If I turned it over, what would I find? Micah was only sixteen, what's the worst he could've been involved with? I'd already decided it was another girl, and I braced myself for it.

Chase sipped his coffee, tea, or whatever it was. I grabbed the cup from him and sniffed it. "Chai tea."

He raised a brow. "What did you think it was?"

"You sipped it like it was hard liquor or something."

"What did you expect me to do, gulp it? It's hot. Are you going to look at the note?" he asked, tapping the paper.

I held a finger up and looked at the barista. "Tasha, can I get a water?" She nodded, and I turned back to Chase. "Why can't you just tell me what it says?"

Tasha placed a plastic cup of water on the counter. I went to get it, then returned to our spot. A reflection in the shiny metallic napkin holder on the table caught my eye. I froze with the cup in my mouth, staring at it.

"What's wrong?" asked Chase. He looked from me to the napkins, then stood and moved beside me. "Is-is it the napkin holder?"

I nodded.

His voice sounded choked. "Brie… You see him too?"

I dropped the cup. Everything went black.

A cold, hard surface pressed against my cheek. I opened my eyes, seeing the concrete floor. Chase knelt beside me and helped me sit up. Tasha crouched next to him.

I looked around. "What happened?"

Chase patted my back. "You tell me. You just toppled over."

"She's okay?" asked Tasha.

He nodded. "Yes."

"Should we call a—"

"No."

Tasha cast me a worried look but straightened and went back to work behind the coffee bar.

So embarrassing. Not only had I realized my dead boyfriend was hanging around on a napkin holder, but I'd fainted in public. I pushed Chase aside, then got to my feet and sat in my chair.

"I'm so sorry." I covered my face.

"What happened?" Chase asked again. He got up and sat across from me.

I placed my hands flat on the table and looked at the napkin holder. It was shiny and new. No Micah.

"What did you say to me? Before I fainted?" I asked, still disoriented.

Chase looked around at those in the coffee shop watching us. "Let's get out of here."

6

Chase's expression held a mix of concern and distress. He grabbed my hand and my bookbag and pulled me outside. We walked across the parking lot and stopped at the crosswalk. I didn't wait for the light to turn. I crossed the street, and Chase followed me.

Normal traffic noises were drowned out by the screeching of brakes and the blaring horns of the cars driving around us. I didn't know where I was going.

In front of the high school, I stopped abruptly, and Chase bumped into me.

"Answer my question." What happened in the coffee shop came back to me—his words before I'd fainted.

The Lincoln High marching band, wearing their black and white uniforms, boarded the school bus in the parking lot as Chase spoke. "It started the night of the funeral. I saw Micah in my mirror."

I crossed my arms. "Me too. Why didn't you tell me?"

"I thought I was going crazy."

"I did too." I rubbed my temple. "Did he talk to you?"

Chase scratched his head. "No. But it doesn't make sense. He's gone, so why is this happening?"

"I don't know. Oh, I got this text too," I pulled my phone from my denim purse and unlocked it. I moved closer to Chase to show him the screen. A group of girls from one of my classes walked by, and I lowered my voice. "See here?"

Chase read the text aloud. "*I'm not where I'm supposed to be.* Is that supposed to be from Micah?"

"I-I don't know."

I sat on a cement parking block in the now-empty parking lot. The last of the student stragglers walked past us—those whose parents forgot to pick them up or who had detention or an afterschool program.

Chase sat beside me and slowly rubbed his hands together as if smoothing a precious piece of wood with sandpaper. "This is beyond bizarre." He looked past me.

I twisted around and looked at the Chinese restaurant across the street. "Oriental Garden."

"What?"

I turned back to him. "We had dinner there one night. My family and Micah." I smiled. It had been a fun evening. "He and my dad got along so well. They kept going off talking by themselves, and I hoped my dad wasn't threatening his life or something. Anyway, I don't know why, but I really do believe the text came from Micah. Oh, wait." I pointed at my phone screen. "Look at the number it came from."

"Yeah, let me see that." Chase took my phone and held it close to his face. He wagged a finger at the phone. "It's him. It has to be."

"How do you know?"

"What was Micah into?"

"Dancing?"

"No, *really* into?"

I paused, thinking. "The metaverse. M&Ms... Wait, computers!"

"Yes. Those numbers. That's binary," said Chase.

"Do you know what it means?" I asked, my eyes wide. I slapped my forehead. "Wait, I've got it. Micah loved video games. We used to play them together all the time." I sucked in a breath and grabbed Chase's arm. "What if he didn't really die, but went to another place?"

Chase shook his head. "Why would you say that?"

"I don't know, but maybe..."

Chase wrinkled his nose. "Maybe what? Where do you think he is?"

It was going to sound absurd, but it made me feel good. Like I'd figured it all out. "The metaverse."

"Brie, the metaverse? It's an online MMO." Chase rolled his eyes. "None of that makes sense. But what does make sense is him trying to contact us."

I nodded. "Yeah, from the metaverse."

"Stop saying that. Seriously." Chase pointed at the phone. "The numbers are a sequence of binary digits. Binary code is what's used to control your computer."

He sighed, clearly seeing that I wasn't getting how this was all connected. "Computer programs are sets of instructions. Each instruction is translated into simple binary codes that activate the central processing unit. All software, music, documents, and any other information that is processed by a computer, is also stored using binary."

I pursed my lips. "So what you're saying is—"

"We need to get to a computer."

"I think the computer lab is still open."

"No." Chase shook his head. "Let's keep this private. The school has access to anything we do on those computers. If this text did come from Micah, he's trying to give us instructions or a clue."

"A clue?"

Chase stood and pulled me to standing. "You live closer. Let's go to your house."

"Why did you say a clue? If Micah is trying to contact us, what do you think it means?"

Chase frowned. "I think it means he needs our help."

7

No one was home yet at my house, which was perfect because it gave me and Chase some privacy. After grabbing my laptop from my bedroom, we took our seats on the couch in the living room.

"Think about it," Chase said as he opened my laptop on the coffee table before us. "If Micah can appear to us, then he can appear to anyone. He chose us, and he chose us for a reason."

I nodded. "Good point."

"He knows we will do whatever it takes to help him."

I was suddenly glad to be talking to someone about seeing Micah. Knowing Chase could see him too gave me some relief. It was proof that I wasn't having a psychotic break.

Chase's fingers moved fast over the keyboard. "I'll start with a search of that code from the message he sent you."

I placed my phone beside him so he could read the numbers from the text. He was good with this stuff. Just like Micah.

Chase looked over at me. "Aren't you, uh, going to eat something? You didn't eat anything at the coffee shop. You're not hungry? No after school snack?"

I rolled my eyes. "I'm fine, Mom."

"I did just sound like a parent, didn't I? But, uh, maybe that's why you fainted, and you're looking a little thin."

"Do I have to eat when I'm not hungry?"

He frowned. "I'm just saying… Micah would want me to look after you."

My jaw clenched, and I jabbed a finger in his direction. "I know what you're trying to say, and you're about to piss me off. I don't do that anymore. Not in over a year. I lost weight from grieving, not from anorexia."

Chase sighed. "Okay. I'm sorry. Micah liked you curvy, I'm just saying. What are you, a size four now?"

I shook my head. "Maybe. Let's change the subject. I'm sorry for raising my voice."

Chase jumped to his feet and pulled me toward the kitchen. "I think Micah would want you to eat."

I yanked my hand from his. "What part of 'not hungry' do you not understand?"

"Resistance is futile."

"Please don't start with the *Star Trek* references." I pointed at my laptop. "What about—"

He raised his brows. "This will only take a minute. What do you have a taste for?"

I relented and followed Chase into the kitchen. He rummaged around in the fridge, opened the vegetable and fruit crisper drawers, and pulled out a carton of strawberries.

"Have you ever had a strawberry and cream cheese sandwich?" He took the berries to the sink and rinsed them.

I hadn't, but it sounded interesting and light. "Toast the bread. Open-faced."

I sat at the kitchen table, eating my strawberry and cream cheese sandwich. Chase went to the living room and grabbed my laptop, then took the seat across from me and opened it.

After only a few minutes, he gave the keyboard a final tap and exclaimed, "Done!"

"What was that, all of three minutes? Let's see what you've got." I stood and rounded the table, then placed my hands on the back of his chair and leaned over it, looking at the screen. "Heaven? Those numbers mean heaven? Are you kidding me? Micah is not in heaven. He says he's not where he's supposed to be, which should be heaven. He didn't have an evil bone in his body. Why isn't he in heaven?"

"Calm down," Chase replied. "First things first. This text was totally from Micah. I believe he was able to utilize tech somehow—through energy or something. He used 'heaven' to get your attention. Now, if he's not there, where is he? And how do we get him home?"

My head tilted. "Home?"

"Heaven."

"You can't get someone there. They have to follow the light or something."

Chase took the paper from his pocket—the one he'd tried to give me at the coffee shop—and handed it to me. "Read."

"Does it have something to do with heaven?" I unfolded the note and read it aloud. "Meet me at the Oak Room. Eleven p.m. About ELF." I looked at Chase. "You were acting all CSI about *this*? I don't get it. Why did this alarm you?"

"The Oak Room is a club."

"Micah didn't go to clubs. Plus, he wasn't old enough."

"And the time."

I glanced at the paper again. "Right, curfew. So who was he meeting there? And what the heck does ELF stand for?"

Chase rubbed his chin. "I don't know. But I have an idea of how we can find out."

"How?"

"Micah's phone and laptop. I have to take the contents of his gym and hall lockers to his parents. I can ask to go to the bathroom, and then go to his bedroom and get them."

"I'm going with you," I said.

My mother walked into the kitchen. At the sight of Chase, her eyes widened and her mouth slightly opened like she was going to say something.

"Hello, Mrs. London," he said.

She glanced at me, at Chase, and back at me. "It's good to see you, Chase. Are you doing all right?"

"Yes, ma'am."

"Good. Let me and Brie have a minute, would you?"

"Sure." Chase got to his feet and left the kitchen.

My mother didn't take her eyes off me as she set her purse and lunch bag on the table. She gestured for me to follow her. "Come."

We went to the family room and sat on the sofa. She looked nice and professional in her suit and short haircut, which made everyone tell her she looked like Halle Berry. I crossed my arms, turning my knees to face her. "Whatever it is, I didn't do it. Talk to Elle about it."

"No, that's not what this is." My mother rubbed her forehead. "Brie, how do I say this without sounding—"

"Just say it."

"Okay." She sighed. "It's not a good idea to rebound with your deceased boyfriend's best friend."

I threw my hands in the air. "Ugh, Mom, no. Is that what you think is happening here? You think I would do that? Chase is my friend too. And Micah hasn't even been gone a month."

My mother shook her head. "What I think is you're very vulnerable, Brie."

"No, I'm not. I can still be friends with Chase."

She patted my forearm. "Honey, I'm not so sure it's the right time."

I jerked it away from her. "I can't just not be friends with him."

"Lower your voice."

"So you think because of Micah I shouldn't have any friends?" I was so sick of everyone treating me like I was so fragile.

My mother's eyes widened. "No, that's not what I'm saying."

I scowled at her. "Yes, you are."

"I'm talking about boys," she replied. "You're both hurting, and things can happen."

"Things like what?"

"Brie..."

"Monica..."

"Brie, we've allowed you to express yourself freely to help you deal with everything you've been going through, but call me by my first name one more time..." She wagged a finger at me. "You're about to get yourself grounded. You know I don't like when you do that."

I knew better. I only called her by her first name to aggravate her the same way she aggravated me.

"I'm sorry," I said. "But you don't have to worry. I'm not even sexually active."

"Did someone say 'sex?'" asked Elle, prancing into the room wearing tie-dyed leggings and a rhinestone-embellished white T-shirt. She clutched her open blue-jean jacket.

"Yeah, Elle, Mom thinks I'm a slut," I got to my feet and wiggled my butt. "Like I'm running down the street holding my skirt up and poking my butt out yelling, 'Come and get it!'"

Elle scrunched up her face. "Why would anybody do that? Gross!"

I'd gone too far, and I knew it. I shook my head, staring at my mother. "I'm sorry."

"Elle, go to your room," my mom said.

Elle stamped her foot. "But I didn't do anything."

My mom pointed at the hallway, and Elle stomped away.

She turned to me, her face creased with worry. "Brie, you've been through so much. I just don't want to see you get hurt. Plus you're only fifteen and—"

"I know, I know, Mom." I waved her off. "I have a full life ahead of me, and there's plenty of boys out there, and there will be time for dating later. Mom,

I'll be fine. It's not like Chase and I are dating. We're just friends."

"You and Micah were just friends once too."

I glared at her, and she held up her hands and said, "Okay. Fine… I said my piece. It still doesn't feel right."

"We're just hanging out."

"I'm still not too keen on it."

"So what would you have me do, kick him out?" I asked.

"No," my mother said. "I guess not. Just be careful."

"I will."

I began to walk away, but my mother grabbed my arm and rubbed it. "Wait. Wait a minute. I'm a grown woman and can admit when I *may* be overreacting."

I raised my head. The fall at the coffee shop must've affected my hearing. *Did she just apologize?*

"Forgive me for being 'that' mom." She smiled. "If you say it's innocent, it's innocent. I trust you. Forgiven?"

"Forgiven," I replied.

She sighed as she stood. "I guess I'll get dinner started."

I followed her to the kitchen, then grabbed my plate and brushed the crumbs from the table onto it before she could find something else to complain about.

"You ate?" she asked.

I nodded. "Have you ever had strawberries and cream cheese on toast? Yum, Mom. Like, no joke."

She grinned. "Interesting. I'll have to make myself one."

I went to the living room and sat on the couch beside Chase. "You didn't hear any of that did you?"

He took an earbud from his ear. "I tried not to. 'Come and get it?'" he chuckled.

"Are you mad?"

He shrugged. "Your mom is just being a mom."

"That's so mature of you. So are you ready to go see Micah's parents?" I asked.

"No. Tomorrow we get out of school early. We'll go then."

8

I sat in class during seventh period, listening to the hum of the fluorescent lights and staring at the back of the student in front of me. Cruz hadn't had a haircut in a while, so his hair grew down the back of his neck. I studied the way the short hairs formed a V down to his collar. The teacher asked a question and a few hands shot up around me, but I didn't know what the question was and didn't care. Once the bell rang, I'd meet up with Chase at my locker, and we'd get on with his plan.

"Gabriella? Gabriella?" Torrie snapped her fingers near my face.

I glanced at her hand and then around me as everyone laughed. "Huh?"

She pointed to the front of the class.

"Office," said the teacher, pointing at the door.

They'd caught me daydreaming, but for once, I hadn't been thinking about Micah. My thoughts had drifted back to what had happened at lunch. The sophomore screw-up had come over to my table with his band of giggling idiots. He'd sat beside me in his oversized jersey and jeans while the others had stood around us.

"Hey Brie," he said. "I know you're dealing with a lot of emotional stuff right now, but I'm trying to understand something I heard. You know how people talk."

I turned to him thinking, *here we go.*

"You stopped eating and almost died, your boyfriend saved your life. I mean, that's what I heard. He gets sick and dies." His eyes narrowed. "But you're still here. I don't get it. Shouldn't you have found some way to save Micah in return?"

His friends giggled. We were in the same classes throughout grade school. Something had happened to him in middle school, and he became angry all the time. I've disliked him ever since.

"I mean, is it fair that you're still here?" he asked.

I pushed back the tears that were forming. *Don't give him the satisfaction*, I told myself. After

Micah's passing, and the passing of other students due to the virus, I would've thought that we all would treat each other better. That we'd all realize life is short, and you never know when it's the last time you will see someone. Why wouldn't that make us come together rather than be at odds with one another?

"Henry!" Shannon shouted from several feet away, her voice cutting through the air. "What the heck was that?" It may have been the first time I heard her voice before the tinkling of her bracelets.

He lifted his hands like he was innocent. "What?"

"Butt wipe, I heard what you just said to her!"

"Dude, she called you butt wipe," said one of his friends, laughing.

Shannon stormed up to Henry's face, close enough to smell his beef jerky breath that had assaulted my nose as he'd spoken to me.

He glowered at her. "Mind your business, Shannon."

She was about to snap, and I appreciated it, but I didn't need defending. Mostly, I didn't want anyone's pity, being the dead guy's girlfriend and all.

Shannon lifted her palm toward me. "Give me the slap certificate, Brie."

I held up my hand, "It's okay."

Shannon backed away, gritting her teeth. Her jaw tensed and twitched.

"Henry Adams, you want to talk about fair? Is it fair that you have a herpes on your lip?" I asked.

"Ooo…" someone said.

His hand shot to his mouth. He wore a tiny hoop earring in his ear, and I wished I could snatch it out. The back and the sides of his head were tapered low. The hair on top was long and hung in six braids to his shoulders. If someone would hold him down, I could loop one of those through the earring and yank it.

Henry dropped his hand and looked at his friends with a smirk. I guess he'd thought up a good retort. His mouth opened to speak just as I stood to deliver the words that would be a punch to his gut.

"Or is it fair that your father is sending flowers to a woman who is not your mother every week?" I smirked. "Yeah, I know. I work at the flower shop. Arthur. That's his name, right? Arthur Adams? You think about that and get back to me." I said and walked away.

"Oh yes, she did!" Shannon said with a hand over her mouth as if someone had first said, 'Oh no, she didn't!'

Maybe that hadn't been the best way for Henry to find out about his father, but what he'd said to me was heartless. At least I'd leaned toward his ear and had lowered my voice when I'd said it. Instead of the whole cafeteria, only those closest to us had heard. Still, no matter how mean he was, I was convicted about my choice of payback. That's the thing about words. You can't take them back.

Now, the teacher jabbed her finger at the door again. I grabbed my books and left the class. Ever since I returned to school, I'd been expecting to be called to the office and was actually surprised it had taken this long.

I strode into Mrs. Westhall's office.

"Hello, Gabriella." She set aside the paperwork she'd been reading and smiled as she looked at me from behind her desk. A lanyard hung from her neck, and she wore a tan fuzzy sweater over her collared shirt.

Mrs. Westhall was biracial, like me. She'd mentioned it when I first met her, as if it connected us in some way. But I was like, who cares? It wasn't like I was the lone biracial teen and had never seen another before. It would've been different had she said that when she was little, her father's form of family time meant her standing on the coffee table and belting out "Nessun dorma" which Luciano Pavarotti's amazing voice made famous—and I only knew that because of my dad—or that her noni got a cell phone recently and was driving her crazy, taking pictures of herself over and over and sending them to her. That would've connected us, I think.

"Please, have a seat," she said, indicating the chair in front of her desk, then went back to leafing through the folder.

A window next to her desk faced the student parking lot, which was now half-empty. To her right sat a table littered with books and files. I took the guest chair directly in front of her and drew in a deep breath.

Noise assaulted us from the hallway—students' and teachers' shuffling feet, classroom doors opening and closing, a few laughs, and a few swear words.

Mrs. Westhall waved at the open door. "Gabriella, please close the door."

I rose, shut it carefully, and sat again.

Mrs. Westhall gave me the usual checklist of questions regarding my feelings and coping mechanisms. She wanted to know how I was dealing with my grief and if I was facing it or running from it. It wasn't like the therapy I received in the outpatient hospital over a year ago, and I was glad. I never really liked the group sessions.

When she was done, I said, "What you really want to know is how the stress is affecting me."

Mrs. Westhall nodded, waiting for me to say more.

"I'm eating. I wasn't at first, but I am now. Ask my parents. Micah would want that."

She leaned forward. "I'm sure Micah would, but do *you* want that? I mean for you?"

"Yes. Like I said, I'm eating."

"Gabriella, you have to move forward."

I slumped in the chair. "I do. I am."

"Really?" She quirked a brow. "I'm not so sure. Can you tell me anything about your life?"

"I work part-time at a flower shop, but they gave me time off to mourn. I'm going to be a junior next year."

"And?"

I shifted uneasily. "And what?"

"What are your plans?"

"I don't know." I shrugged. "To go to college one day. To get a job that pays more to help me start saving for college, I guess. Does every fifteen-year-old know every step of their future?"

"No," Mrs. Westhall replied. "But I like that you've thought about yours. And if you work on improving your grades, maybe you can get a scholarship to college."

I nodded.

"As you know, there's a support group for students out back," she said, pointing behind her. "They meet once a week. You could really benefit from it, you know?"

"Yeah, I know. Thanks."

She steepled her fingers. "It's okay if you don't think it's right for you right now, I just want you to know that's an option."

I pressed my lips together. "I know. Thanks."

"Brie, you have my card. Call me at any time."

"Thanks." I got up to leave.

I'm sure my parents will, like they did this time.

I met Chase outside a few minutes later.

"Where have you been?" he asked with his hands on his hips. "I've already seen Micah three times today."

I glanced around at the other students leaving for the day. "Lower your voice before someone thinks you're nuts. That's why I keep my head down when I walk. Keep your eyes on your sneakers. Anyway, I got called to Mrs. Westhall's office."

Chase zipped his jacket. "Well, Micah had the nerve to show up in the lenses of Mr. Phelpson's glasses. I looked like a complete idiot staring at him with my eyes all bugged out. But regarding Mrs. Westhall, everyone is getting called down to see her. They're making the rounds to anyone who was friends with Micah, or on a team, or in a club with him. Did it go okay?"

"I guess."

He gave me a sympathetic nod. "All right, well, let's get going. Maximum warp. Punch it."

I rolled my eyes. "Chase, really, what's with you and the *Star Trek* references all the time?"

He grinned as we began to walk toward Micah's house. "I'm a huge *Star Trek* fan. Hardcore. A better question is, how do you know they're *Star Trek* references? Do I detect a low-key Trekker?"

I snorted. "No comment."

We talked most of the way but stopped when we turned onto Micah's block. I closed my eyes and opened them again. It was still there. That familiar feeling. The frustration. The dread. It was the same as the day he'd passed.

I imagined Micah in the street throwing a football to Chase while I sat on the front steps, getting my hair french braided by his sister.

I looked at Chase and ran a hand in front of his face.

He sniffed and wiped away the tear threatening to fall from his eye. "I'm okay," he said, blinking and shaking his head, coming out of his own thoughts. The wetness in his eyes made them shine like polished stones.

Chase turned and crossed the street toward the two-story white house. But I stayed right where he left me on the curb.

He frowned and crossed back to me. "What is it?"

"I don't know." I looked up and down the block. Everything was quiet. Peaceful. There were no signs of anything out of the ordinary. Chase followed me as I crossed. "I don't know if I can go in," I said, stopping at the front steps of Micah's house.

"I feel you," he replied, gently touching my shoulder. "But we can. We have to. We owe it to ourselves to find out what was really going on with our friend. We were his best friends. He told us everything, but not this? It doesn't add up."

I shifted uneasily. "I know you're right, but still..."

Chase walked up the three cement steps to the front door, rang the doorbell, and then knocked. The door hadn't been closed all the way, and slowly opened as if blown by a gentle wind. He looked at me, and I shrugged.

"Hello?" he called, then pushed the door fully open and started inside.

"We're going in?" I asked. He didn't reply, so I hopped up the steps and inside after him.

The house was quiet except for a slight hum from the refrigerator. It was a small house for such a large family but filled with so much love. We walked into the dining room.

"Hello?" came a voice from the kitchen.

"Hey, it's Chase," he replied.

Micah's mother came around the corner, holding a stack of papers in her arms. At the sight of us, she dropped everything on the dining room table. Like a bird of prey, she swooped down, scooped up Chase, and squeezed him as tight as she could. Then she gave me a second look and broke into tears as she reached for me.

"Brie, I didn't think I'd ever see you again," she said with a sob. "You know you're like a daughter to me. You're always welcome here."

"Yes," I said as I hugged her back. Mrs. George was a hugger, so I was used to getting them from her, but her hug didn't feel the same as before. She was thinner now—frail even. "You've always told me that."

"Are you hungry?" she asked, pulling away and straightening her blouse. "I can heat you up something."

Most likely, she'd cooked oxtails and rice. She was an amazing cook of things I'd never heard of like roti, aki and saltfish—all from her Caribbean background.

Chase shook his head and held out the bag full of Micah's belongings. "No, we came by to bring you Micah's things."

Mrs. George eyed the bag but didn't take it.

Chase and I exchanged glances. He held the bag up and gestured for me to say something.

"Uh, Mrs. George, do you think we could take it up to his room?" I asked.

She exhaled. "Thank you. That would be nice."

I got the feeling Mrs. George hadn't gone into Micah's room since his passing.

"Would it be okay if we stayed up there a bit and just…" I wasn't sure of what to say, but she nodded.

"Take all the time you need."

As we walked down the hall, I found myself looking around, trying to take it all in. Everything looked exactly as I last saw it—everything except for one wall now covered in black framed photos of Micah from a baby to this year.

Chase stopped outside Micah's closed bedroom door. We stood there, staring at it for a long time. One of Micah's younger siblings had drawn a picture of the family and taped it on the door. *I miss you* was written on the bottom in scribbled handwriting.

"This is it," said Chase, giving me a serious look. "Ready?"

I sucked in a breath. "As I'll ever be."

I couldn't bring myself to open the door, so Chase turned the knob and slowly pushed it open.

It was the smell that hit me first—the same smell of all Micah's clothes. My eyes watered. It was faint, but still there. Cool Waters cologne, Axe deodorant. I choked up and turned away.

"It's stuffy in here. I-I'll open the window."

I stood there a moment, watching cars pass by and thinking of Micah. My back was turned to

Chase, but I heard him sniff. All the things in this room—mementos from places we'd been, including a glass turtle I'd stolen on a whim from a table at the Wilhurst flea market, then regretted. Especially after Micah's thou-shalt-not-steal lecture.

Just so many memories, including the time Micah snuck me in when his mother wasn't home. First, he'd hung out in the back room of the flower shop, doing homework until I got off work. Then, he'd asked me if I wanted to hang out at his house. I hadn't wanted to. I'd known his mother's rules. But Micah had dared me, and I never backed down from a dare. I'd almost eaten a roach once as a kid because of a dare. My mother had walked in just in time. "Gabriella Lola London, don't you dare!" Anyway, it had ended up being a delightful afternoon goofing around with Micah's younger siblings. We'd even cooked dinner together, with Micah revealing the secret ingredient in his spaghetti sauce—hot sauce.

Micah's bedroom looked exactly the same as the last time I'd been there. Nothing was out of place.

I pulled the curtain open more and waved my hand at the dust flying into my face. I was close enough to the window to see the faint reflection of my waist, and beside it was Micah's. Only this time, instead of facing the same direction as me, his body was turned to the right.

What is it? Why are you turned away? Is there something over there? I darted my gaze around Micah's room, looking for anything out of the ordinary.

Then, I looked beside me and to the right, and I saw something flat sticking out from beneath the curtain resting on the edge of his dresser. "Chase, come here," I said. "What's this?"

"What do you see?" Chase hurried over, pushed the curtain aside and pulled at the object. "It's taped. It's an envelope. Help me."

We carefully pulled one end of the dresser from the wall, while holding the small television on top of it.

Chase worked at peeling the envelope from the back of the dresser. "Man, this is taped down good. There's two of them."

I grabbed scissors from a jar of pens on top of the dresser. "Cut it so you don't tear the envelope."

He took the scissors and nodded, then used them to cut the tape. "Got it!"

We stood shoulder to shoulder as he opened the first large manilla envelope.

It was filled with money. Our mouths dropped.

"Where did he get that?" I asked as Chase flipped through the bills.

"Micah had a job. Maybe he was saving up," Chase replied, I think trying to convince himself.

"Yeah, but we do that in banks," I replied. "Why was he hiding it?"

"Maybe because it's stacks of hundred-dollar bills." Chase's eyes grew wide. "I bet this is over fifty grand. I'm putting it back."

"No, give it to his family. They need it."

Chase's brows furrowed. "Why wouldn't he have given it to them? Micah would help anyone, you know that. Especially his family. Brie, think about it. What are they going to say when they see it? 'Where in the world did Micah get this kind of money?' Then they'll think he was selling dope or something."

I bit my lip. "Well? Was he?"

Chase huffed. "You know better than that."

I shrugged. He had a point. I did know better, but the evidence was starting to take a turn against Micah's character.

I glanced around, then gestured at the computer sitting on the floor in front of the nightstand. "Look, there's his laptop."

Chase picked it up, then looked inside the box on Micah's bed. He sat next to it and pulled out a cell phone. "His phone is here with his things from the hospital."

"Is it charged?" I asked.

"I'm about to find out." He pushed the button on the side and slammed it on his lap. "Dead."

I spotted the charge cord on the nightstand, then walked over and handed the end of it to Chase. "There. The charger is right here behind the lamp."

Chase plugged the phone in. "Okay," he said, turning on the laptop. He cracked his knuckles. "Oh, I forgot about the password."

I sat beside him. "Any ideas?"

"What did he and I have in common?"

"Hacking," he answered his own question. Twice, he tried typing in combinations of letters and numbers, neither of which worked. Then, on the third attempt, he let out a gleeful shout. "In!"

"No way. That was too quick. How?"

Chase grinned. "123456."

"Micah couldn't have—"

"I'm joking, but that is the most common password other than the actual word 'password.'"

"I don't even want to know how you've tested that to confirm it." I shook my head. "The less I know, the less information I'll have for the police when they interrogate me."

"Ha! No." Chase gestured at the screen. "Really, it was his two favorite people. You and his baby brother. Gabby and Trent backward and your birth years."

I bumped his shoulder with mine. "You were his favorite too."

He scoffed. "I'm a realist. I know I come after the parents and all the siblings."

"Okay, whatever, go to his emails."

Chase clicked on the icon, and the emails opened without him needing to log in. "It's weird that he left this open. Like he may have wanted to make sure someone could get to it."

Chase read through a bunch of the emails while I looked around the room. I focused on Micah's favorite picture of me downtown on a turquoise bike. It was the way I'd looked back at him, he'd said, that made him love the photo so much.

Chase gasped. "Wait, there's—"

I spun around. "What?"

"Micah hacked into—where is this going? Mic...
Nooooo!" Chase's eyes bulged, and he covered his mouth as he spoke.

I went to his side. "What is it?"

"Raul Witman." Chase's voice shook. "Micah hacked into Raul's whole system. You know who that is right? He runs the city. The underground anyway. Drugs—all kinds of illegal stuff."

I knew the name. It ignited fear in anyone who lived on the south side. "I don't understand. Why would Micah hack into Raul's computers? What was he doing?"

Chase took an external drive from his pocket and plugged it into the laptop. "Looking for something, I guess. I don't know, but Raul isn't someone you want to mess with. Maybe he was trying to stop him. But that doesn't make sense either. I don't know. Wait a minute." Chase's eyes narrowed at the screen. "He was trying to get information about some girl."

My chest pinched. "What girl?"

9

I knew it. There *was* someone else. I bet it was that hoochie, Tamala, who had always been hanging around, smiling into his face and drooling all over him. I could hear her voice in my head now. "Oh Micah, you're such an amazing artist, I bet you could draw me so well," she'd said as she poked her bajungas out at him. I remember looking down at my A-cups that night in my mirror and practicing poking them out like that. It had done nothing for me.

My heart pounded. *How could Micah do this to me? If he wasn't dead already, I'd kill him.* My stomach lurched, and I clasped it. I was going to be sick.

"Let's see here," said Chase, still looking at the screen. "There was a girl who went missing about a month before Micah got the virus. Her face was plastered all over the city—store windows, the newspapers, the news. I don't remember her name, but I remember her face because she looked like you."

It's about a missing person's case? Way to overreact, Gabriella. I let out a sigh of relief. "I sort of remember that. What was her name?"

Chase right-clicked on her photo and selected from the menu on the search engine to show him everywhere it could find that image.

Several photos of her of different sizes appeared on the right side of the screen. On the left, news articles and blog posts about her popped up.

Chase tapped his chin, leaning closer to the laptop. "Let me see. She has ASD. Didn't know that…" He scrolled down. "Emily. Emily L. Fulton."

I stood up, confused.

Chase craned his neck to look at me. "Brie, what's wrong?"

"Nothing, it's just I know that name for some reason. Emily…" I frowned. "I can't remember why."

"Maybe because you saw a news report with her mother pleading for the kidnapper to let her go."

"Chase, say her whole name again."

"Emily L. Ful—" He gasped. "ELF!"

"ELF is her!" I exclaimed.

"Yes, and don't ask me what it means because I have no answers." Chase turned the screen to me and zoomed in. Below a missing person's report was a photograph of a girl who looked a lot like me. Shorter hair, but the same color and texture. Same eyes. Similar olive complexion.

I glanced at Chase. "She does kind of look like me."

"Kind of? You should do a DNA test. I'm telling you, she's kin. I'll take this home and see what else I can dig up," he said, pointing at the external drive.

He glanced at the phone on the nightstand. "Micah's phone has a little juice. Let's try it. This one I know the password to, because he let me use it before."

"Wait a minute." I held up a finger. "It's the same as the laptop password, isn't it? That's how you got into the laptop so quickly. You already knew it."

Chase grinned. "Not at first, but then I thought, let me try the phone password just in case." He grabbed the phone, entered the password, and then drew a pattern on the screen. It unlocked. "Okay, and now I'm going to the texts."

I waited anxiously with my arms crossed over my chest, squeezing them. Micah's mother had to be wondering what was taking us so long. Then again, maybe not. The room felt like him. Even if we weren't investigating, we would've stayed a while, just looking around.

"Oh-oh," Chase said, staring at the phone screen.

"What?"

"Nothing." He set the phone on his lap, then shut down the laptop and put it back on the ground where we found it.

"Are you crazy?" I demanded. "This is what I came here for! To see if the text came from Micah." I held out my hand. "Give me the phone."

"Brie, I don't think—"

"Give it here."

Chase gave me his hardest stare.

"Two to the throat," I said, making a chopping motion. "You know how I do." I moved toward him in a threatening stance.

"Oh for the love of—here." Chase handed the phone to me.

I swiped through Micah's texts and stopped on *Lorenzo London*. My breath caught. *My father?* "Huh?"

I tapped the text and read:

Lorenzo: I don't know when they will do it, but they will. You have to keep an eye on her until I come up with it.

Micah: I will.

Lorenzo: Thank you for keeping my secret. My children don't know.

Micah: You should talk to them, sir. It would help.

Lorenzo: I don't want them to see me any differently. Please don't say anything to Brie.

Micah: You should tell her.

Lorenzo: I can't.

Lorenzo: I just want to keep her safe.

Micah: Then take her away.

Lorenzo: They're already watching everything I do. This is the only way to keep her from being taken.

Micah: I won't let that happen. If we can hold out until winter break, we can take a trip.

"What did he mean by taken?" I asked, looking at Chase.

Chase didn't respond.

"What did he mean?" I asked again.

But I knew.

Suddenly, the air was too thick. I couldn't breathe. Everything in Micah's room was closing in on me. I dropped the phone, ran down the hallway, and out the front door.

I stood in the sun, my heart racing. In my mind, I ran through every sort of ridiculous scenario. The one that stuck, though, was this—Micah and my father were working together to protect me. Raul had seen me somehow, thought I was gorgeous, and threatened to kidnap me. But why me when there were thousands of attractive girls out there? And ones of legal age? Not that they should be taken either, I mean...I don't know what I meant.

A few minutes later, Chase came out of the house and found me at the curb. My hands on my hips, as I stepped back and forth, taking deep breaths.

"Are you okay?" He placed a hand on my back.

I nodded, still feeling like I might hyperventilate, and at the same time wishing I had a rubber band to shoot him in the face with.

Chase hugged me. "Don't worry, Micah's mother thinks you were just overcome with emotion."

"Okay, good," I replied. "Those texts, though. They're talking about me, aren't they?" I knew they were. I just needed him to say it.

He squeezed me again. "We can't talk here. Micah's mother is watching from the window. Come on."

He let me go, and I lumbered up the block after him. As soon as we were out of sight of Micah's house, I stopped.

"I can't do this. I don't want to know what was going on anymore."

Chase's mouth fell open. "What? Brie, we have to keep digging. We're just getting started. Do you want to figure out what really happened or not? Micah is leading us to clues. It's not what everyone thinks."

"What's not?" I demanded. "What is it that you think really happened?"

Chase glanced around us, as if to make sure nobody was listening. "I'm starting to think Micah was murdered."

"No, that's impossible. He caught the virus, and he had a bad heart that no one knew about."

"Keep telling yourself that," Chase replied, walking away.

I marched after him. "No. I don't believe it. You can't just turn my life into some murder mystery."

Chase spun around. "Brie, stop being naive. An envelope full of cash? Excuse me, two envelopes full of cash. Hacking into Raul Whitman's system? ELF? The texts from your dad? Wait. Oh my gosh..."

He turned away from me and hurried down the sidewalk again.

"What? What is it?" I asked as I followed him.

"Nothing. Go home."

Chase jogged off, putting some distance between us. I followed him, jogging every other step but keeping out of his sight. I watched as he took a path through a hedge of trees, and I stayed a few dozen feet behind him. When Chase got to his front door, he went inside and closed it behind him. I waited, wondering what he was doing inside. Finally, I tried the knob, found it unlocked, and stormed inside. I found him in the kitchen.

"What?" I demanded, slamming my purse on the counter.

He whirled around, scowling. "You just walked into my house?"

I scowled right back at him. "No. I broke in."

Chase stared at me.

I pointed behind me. "You left the door open."

Chase walked quickly through the house, as if he could lose me by doing so. I walked just as quickly after him and followed him to the home office. Four screens lined the wall in front of the computer desk. Two mice and two keyboards sat on the desktop. Each monitor was about the size of a small laptop screen. He sat at the desk, turned on the computer, and inserted the external drive.

He glanced at me. "I'm going to retrace his steps."

My voice shook. "You are not about to do the same thing Micah did."

He clenched his jaw. "Oh, yes, I am. I'm going to find out what really happened to him. Micah mattered. To his family. To me. And to you."

My stomach roiled. "Chase, really, don't do it. I have a bad feeling about it."

"I have to be sure." He waved at the door. "Go home, Brie. Just go home."

I stood my ground. "I'm not going anywhere."

He slammed his fist on the computer desk. "Didn't you hear me? I said go home!"

10

"No!" I refused to budge. Who the heck did Chase think he was talking to, raising his voice like that? We'd been friends a long time, so he knew me. I would haul off and pop him.

Chase turned around, sneered at me, and then went back to the computer screen.

"Fine. It's your funer—"

"Excuse me?"

"I didn't mean that," he grumbled.

I went to the next room to give Chase a moment to calm down (well, not just him), all the while calling him names in my head that I'd never say aloud. Their family room had a loft seating area where I remembered us all sitting around and eating pizza with pepperoni and pineapple on it. That combination of toppings had been so weird to me, but Chase and Micah loved it.

I leaned against the wall and thought about ELF, listening to Chase tap away on the keyboard. *Emily L. Fulton. What were you doing Micah?*

Chase murmured something I couldn't make out. I peeked my head into the office, where he talked quietly to himself.

He touched the far left computer screen. "Look at that. The numbers go back seven years."

I stepped through the doorway.

Chase looked over his shoulder and waved me over. He scooted back from the desk, so I could get a good look. Spreadsheets filled with numbers covered all four computer screens.

"Brie, look. That's your father's debt." Chase glanced at me and back at the screen. "Did you know?"

My throat felt tight. "How would I know? Debt for what?"

"Let's find out." Chase kept digging, his fingers moving fast over the keyboard. I wondered if it occurred to him that we hadn't seen Micah's reflection since we started finding all of this stuff out.

"Gambling," said Chase, still staring at the closest screen.

I leaned closer to it and looked at my father's name in the search field. The results showed a calendar going back seven years, with all of his debt listed from various bookies.

"But my father doesn't—wait a minute. Did you say seven years?" A strange feeling came over me. Really, a vague memory. I knew it was true. "That's why my parents were fighting and having problems. I was eight. I didn't know what it was all about. That's why they were divorcing. Because of my dad's gambling debts."

"The ledger shows it stopped for a while." Chase tapped a line on the screen. "His debts were paid in full, and then he must've started up again."

"And he had no way to pay, so he asked Micah for money?"

"No, I don't think so." Chase took out Micah's phone again. "There's nothing in Micah's texts or emails about money."

"Then how did they expect him to pay?" I asked. Chase looked at me askance.

"Me? That's like, real? Like, people really do that?" It wasn't a question, but a realization.

"Don't say I didn't try to spare you from learning all of this." He ran his hand down the column of a spreadsheet. "Brie, it still shows a balance. Meaning, Raul still wants payment."

My eyes widened. "What does that mean?"

"Payment of his debt with money, or they take you for payment."

"This isn't real," I said, shaking my head in horror.

"They're not playing," Chase said. "They'll try to kidnap you. I don't think they're going to stop until they get you."

I gripped the back of his chair for balance. "We need to go to the police."

Suddenly, there was a loud popping sound, and Chase's window cracked. We both stared at it.

I gulped. "Was that him? Micah? Is he trying to tell us something, or do your windows crack on a regular basis?"

Chase got up and looked out the window. "Crap."

The word was accompanied by a curse that had to be one of Chase's inventions, because I'd never heard it before.

"We need to go," he said.

"Now?" I asked, trying to see around him and out the window.

He pushed past me. "Right now."

He threw some items into his backpack as I peeked out the window. A black truck was parked in front of Chase's house, and several men got out of it. "Do you know those men? They're getting out of the truck."

Chase grabbed my arm and pulled me down the hall and out the back door. He held a finger to his lips, then we crept through his backyard, and he hoisted me over the fence.

"Let's go to my house," I whispered as we hurried around the side of his neighbor's home.

We reached the sidewalk, and Chase shook his head gravely as we rushed away. "We can't. How do you think they knew to come to mine?"

I gripped his arm. "They're following us?"

"Or this," he said. He stepped into the street and threw Micah's phone into the back of a passing pickup truck filled with tree limbs.

"Hey, we need that for proof!"

"I've got the proof," Chase replied, holding up the external drive.

Chase and I were on the run like a couple of teens in a bad B movie. We stayed off the main roads, running through yards and down alleys.

"Where are we going?" I asked.

"We've got to keep moving."

Chase ran much faster than I could. He was already half a block ahead of me when I finally stopped for a moment to catch my breath. I was scared out of my mind, and so tired. My lungs and my legs were burning in ways I'd never felt.

Chase stopped and glanced over his shoulder at me. He rounded back and gripped my elbow, urging me on.

"I can't go any further," I said.

"I know. I have an idea. This way." He steered me toward a subway entrance.

We hurried down the two flights of steps and hid in the tunnel. A train rumbled through it behind us, vibrating the wall we leaned against.

I caught my breath, glad to have a break from running. I glanced beside me at Chase. "Chase, where's the money?"

"Right here," he said, patting his backpack.

"Why did you take it?"

"We might need it."

"Did you count it?" I asked. "Is it enough to clear my dad?"

He grunted. "I'm not worried about your dad. I want it to clear you. I'm going to take it to Raul."

Panic shot through me. "No, you're not. I've heard about the things he's done. You're not going there. He'll hurt you."

"Why? He doesn't even know me."

I swatted his arm. "Evidently he does, or those men wouldn't have come to your house."

Chase huffed. "They came to my house because the phone was charged. When it was dead, they couldn't track it. And don't argue with me. I have to take the money to him, Brie. I think that's why Micah had it."

"But where did he get it from? I still want to know." A train clattered past us. I waited for the area to quiet again. "Listen, there's an alley behind my house. When it gets dark, we can go there."

We waited in the subway tunnel for over an hour, sitting on that disgusting platform. The echo of distant trains speeding through other tunnels surrounded us. The stench of mold, stale air, and sewage lingered in the air. My knees kept bouncing up and down, and Chase kept telling me to relax.

"They'll never think to look down here," he told me.

I covered my head with my jacket, a way of giving myself privacy so I could think. Another train rumbled by as I texted Elle:

Me: Tell me when Mom and Dad are not around, so I can come in the back door. Make sure the lights are off in the kitchen.

Elle: Roger that.

I loved that girl. No questions. Just happy to help me and be part of whatever I was doing.

After Chase and I finally decided to leave the subway, we hurried down an uneven back road beneath a thick layer of clouds and a hint of moon. Covering our heads with our hoods, we darted from one shadow to the next. We passed a chain-link fence covered in vines that separated the alley from neighboring homes and the cars and bicycles parked in front of the fence. Power lines buzzed above us as our feet crunched on the gravel road, which sloped gently downward as we walked.

Through the leaves of the shrubs in my backyard, my house looked dark and desolate. Elle had turned off all the lights as instructed. I texted her, and the back door crept open.

We slipped inside as quietly as possible.

"What's going on?" Elle greeted us. She grabbed my hands. "Ooo, you're cold."

I peeked out the window toward the front of our neighbor's house. "How long has that SUV been out there?"

Elle shrugged. "How would I know? I'm not a cat slinking around on windowsills all day."

"Where are Mom and Dad?" I glanced toward the living room. The only light came from the air freshener plugged into the socket in the hallway.

"Mom's upstairs laying down. Dad went out."

I glanced at Chase. "Where?"

"I don't know," Elle replied. "He didn't say. Why are you so worried?"

"It's nothing."

"I need a computer," said Chase.

"You're lying," said Elle, crossing her arms. "You need to tell me what's happening. Why do you keep looking out the window? Why are we standing in the dark? And why does he need a computer? I'm the one covering for you. Why do you think Mom isn't blowing up your phone? Huh? I told her you were with Shannon after school. And she was happy you were somewhere besides with him." She pointed at Chase.

My chest squeezed. "You did that for me?"

"I did that for *me*. I didn't want Mom to come home and freak out. Especially when she and Dad are arguing. She doesn't need the stress."

I frowned. "They're arguing?"

"Yeah, that's why he left." She stepped in front of me, blocking me off from the hall. "So what's going on? And don't lie."

I glanced away from her. "It's nothing."

She held her ground. "You're lying to me."

"It's nothing. I'm not lying."

"It's something. You are."

I shined the dim light from my phone on her. "I'm not."

"Oh yeah, you are." Elle lifted her nose. "Tell me."

"She's just like you," said Chase. "You might as well tell her."

My stomach clenched. "She wouldn't understand."

"Try me," said Elle.

"You're nine years old."

She smirked. "And highly intelligent. Tell."

"You'll think it's too crazy," I said.

"How do you know? You haven't told me yet."

"You wouldn't understand," I said.

"You said that already, and we're going to keep going in circles until you tell me," Elle insisted.

I heaved a sigh and walked down the hall to the living room. She and Chase followed me.

"I'm not going to tell you, Elle," I hissed.

Chase let out an impatient huff. "Oh for heaven's sake. We think Micah is trapped somewhere between heaven and earth, because we've both seen him. We found a wad of money that belonged to him and information about that girl that was missing not too long ago. And something was going on with Micah and your father. They were texting each other. It seems your father might owe some very bad people a lot of money, and I think they followed us today. Oh, and they want to kidnap Brie," he rattled off in one breath.

We were all silent for a moment. Elle shined her phone on Chase's face and looked him in the eye.

My eyes widened and I slapped his arm. "Really? I can't believe you. All you had to say was someone followed us. What the heck is wrong with you? She's nine."

"And a half," Elle said, still looking Chase in the eye.

"Well?" asked Chase.

"I believe you," she said slowly. "You should've come to me from the start."

He raised his brows. "Excuse me?"

"Kids hear everything. We just don't let on that we do."

I took her by the shoulders and turned her to face me. "What do you know?" I asked. "And lower your voice."

"I didn't know everything," she replied, her voice barely above a whisper. "I knew there was something going on, but I didn't know the whole story. Mom and Dad were arguing—something about taking a second mortgage on the house.

"And Micah and Dad, I saw them getting all chummy. There's a guy they both didn't like. I'm guessing he's the bad person you were talking about. When we all went to Happy's Pizza, they thought I wasn't listening near the Ms. Pac-Man machine. They shouldn't have been standing so close to me. I could still hear them over the music, sound effects, and Ms. Pac-Man's waka-waka chomping sounds. Chase," she looked at him, "I had the high score that night, eating power pellets. I was like 'take that, you ghosts,' as I ate them and—"

I squeezed her shoulders. "Elle! What did you hear?"

"I was getting to that. Micah said he was going to get the money from some guy's account."

"Are you sure?" Chase asked.

She nodded. "I needed more quarters, and you know Dad doesn't like it when I interrupt, so I waited. When they saw me, they shut up, but it was too late. I held out my hand and said, 'quarters please.' So they thought I didn't hear anything."

"She's a legit spy," Chase said with awe.

"Thank you." She smiled. "Someone finally appreciates me. I'll get Brie's laptop. Don't do anything until I come back." Elle pulled away from me and hurried upstairs.

Chase shook his head and plopped onto the couch. "Unbelievable. We should've come to her in the first place. Crazy."

I rubbed my forehead. "Chase, what about your parents?"

"They're gone for the weekend. Some convention for my dad's job. That means we have to get this solved immediately. Plus, we need to help Micah move on from wherever he is and doing that depends on everything we're finding out."

Elle returned with my laptop and set it on the coffee table. The three of us sat around it.

Chase inserted the drive. "Your security on this thing sucks."

I shrugged. "Well, I don't really have anything a hacker would want on here, so there's that."

"There's an encrypted video here," he said.

"Can you open it?"

"It may be possible to access the original video data. Do you know a hacker?" He shot me a grin.

I pushed his shoulder. "Ha ha, just get to work."

An hour later, Elle and I had made sandwiches, and she was happy to see me eating. Chase had moved to the kitchen table, which was further from my mom's room, in case she woke up. We sat with him as he worked with my laptop.

114

"Okay," he said, tapping the laptop's touchpad. "It's a little blurry, but this is the best I can do quickly."

We all watched the screen.

Micah was in his bedroom, and his camera or phone was set up across the room.

"If you're seeing this," he said, "Chase got a hold of the video somehow. And I'm guessing he figured out my plan."

Even blurry, it was hard to watch and listen to Micah without tearing up.

Micah paced in front of his bed. "The answer to the question that's got you stumped is cryptocurrency. Yep. I hacked into Raul Witman's cryptocurrency wallet, and it was fun watching his money man squirm with worry over the security of their system.

"I sent them a fake replacement for the system, warning them that their original was vulnerable. He only had to plug the device into a computer and input their crypto wallet recovery key. Once the keys were entered, they were recorded and transmitted to me. I was then able to unlock the wallet on the blockchain, allowing me to siphon funds. But I didn't take any more than what was needed by Mr.

London to pay off his debt and to pay the guy who helped me. He shall remain nameless."

Elle squinted. "I don't know what any of that meant."

I nudged Chase. "Was that you, Chase?"

He shook his head. "Of course not. I'm just finding out about all of this like you. But wow, that was genius."

Micah picked up the picture of me he kept on his nightstand. "If you're watching this, something happened to me. Something bad. I-I just want you to know why I did it. I was only trying to keep Gabby safe. I don't want to imagine what Raul would do to her. I didn't know if he wanted her to hold for ransom, or something worse." His voice cracked. "I'm glad Mr. London came to me. He was honest. Tell Gabby not to hate him. We all make mistakes; we just don't know everyone's dirt. Mr. London didn't know I did this. I acted on my own. We're meeting up for pizza tonight. I'm going to talk to him and give him the money."

He coughed into his fist and broke off for a few seconds. "Excuse me, I think I'm catching a cold." He cleared his throat. "If I know you Chase, and I think I do, you've shown this to Gabby. So Gabby, I'll talk directly to you. Cover your ears, Chase. Are they covered?" Micah asked with a grin. "Gabby, I don't know what's going to happen, but if there's a chance I might die, I just want to say ... I love you."

I hit stop and stared at the screen.

"Wait. There might be more," said Elle. "Hit play."

I couldn't make myself do it.

Chase rewound the video some and pushed play.

Micah's voice came again. "I love you." He paused. "I love you, Gabby. That's right. I'll shout it to the world. I'm sorry for being so stupid. If anything happens to me, promise me you'll keep in touch with Chase and help him through it. He's a good guy."

"I promise," I whispered.

"I love you, Gabby. I love you."

I heard the sound of Micah's bedroom door opening, and he looked away. The screen faded to black.

Chase turned to my sister. "Elle, you said Micah told your dad he was going to get money from some guy's account. Micah just said, 'I'm going to talk to Mr. London tonight and give him the money,' so that was the same night you went to Happy's Pizza." Chase thought for a moment. "He only told him he was going to. He didn't tell him he already had." He turned his gaze to me. "Brie..."

I finally exhaled. "Rewind that."

"No, don't watch it again."

Elle reached over and tapped the back arrow. "It's her laptop. She can do what she wants."

Micah looked away from the screen.

"Listen," I said. "Sh-ah. Did you hear that? There's no one in his family with those syllables."

Chase straightened. "Rewind it again. Sh-aw. It sounds like... Shaw?"

I listened again. "Sh-aw. Shaun. Oh my gosh." I pulled my phone from my pocket, tapped it open, and pulled up my social media. I turned the screen to show Chase. "Look. Shaun Murphy. He sent me a friend request after Micah died. Do you know who that is?"

"I don't," said Chase. "Wait, the only Shaun I know is a tattoo guy."

"You mean he's not a teen?"

"He is, but he does tattoos. I haven't seen him around in a while. I mean, if it's him. He's not the only Shaun around."

A rock formed in the pit of my stomach. "What would he want with me?"

"I don't know—but I know a good way to find out." Chase took my phone and sent Shaun a direct message:

Me: Who are you? Do I know you?

He waited, peering at the screen. "Let's see what he responds."

Elle fell asleep while we waited, leaning on my shoulder and breathing softly as Chase and I talked late into the night.

"How did your parents meet?" he asked, his hands clasped between his knees.

"They met in college in the dining hall," I replied. "There's a whole forbidden love story that you'd have to hear my dad tell or hear my parents tell together. I'd only butcher it. They went through a lot to be together. I'm not sure how he convinced my grandmother to let him marry my mom, but I'm grateful that he did, or I wouldn't be here. I'm named after her. My Italian side. I'm one-fourth Italian."

"Ah, that explains your feistiness."

"That's what they say."

We were silent for a while. I took a deep breath, bracing myself for the question I knew was coming.

"Remember when we went to homecoming last year?" Chase asked.

That wasn't it. I thought he was going to ask for details about how Micah and I had become a couple.

"Ooo, you took Lacey to the dance. And she wore that tight miniskirt."

Chase chuckled. "Yeah, the dreaded miniskirt. Worst date ever. She couldn't even sit. What made her think that was a good idea?"

I snorted. "The internet. That's what it's designed to do—get you to buy stuff."

"Then that was an internet fail."

"Whatever happened to you guys?"

He sighed. "We broke up not long after homecoming. She was too shallow. I couldn't deal with it no matter how cute she was."

I chuckled. "Too many selfies."

"All day long, every day."

I gave him a sympathetic look. "I know that was over a year ago, but sorry it was such a bad night."

"But it wasn't for you and Micah. You stayed out past curfew."

"My mom was pissed. She waited up for me and was like, 'Get your little hot tail in this house,'" I replied, mimicking her voice.

Chase grinned. "Micah got in trouble too."

I pursed my lips. "Yeah, because my mother called his mother."

"I was with him," Chase said. "We dropped Lacey off and went to his house. His mother told him there were so many girls out there, and he couldn't allow himself to get enamored with just one. And do you know what he said?"

"What did he say?"

Chase smiled. "He said, 'There's only one girl for me.'"

I blushed.

"That's why I know this is real," he continued. "You weren't just a school crush, Brie. Mic really loved you."

I cleared my throat. "You know what? I'm going to help you out. I'm going to introduce you to one of my girls."

"Don't bother, your girls are ugly."

I choked on my spit and laughed.

He waved me off. "See that's why you're laughing, because you know I'm telling the truth. You're the cute girl with the ugly friends."

"That is not true. Morgan is not ugly."

"You know what she looks like? Remember that mangy dog we saw downtown that time? His hair stuck up on top like he needed his weave redone. That's Morgan."

I swatted his arm. "Stop it. You're wrong for that. There's Shannon—"

"Have I done something to you that would make you hate me, Brie? That girl is nuts."

We went on like that for another hour. Me mentioning which friend or any girl at school I thought Chase could date, and him telling me what they looked like. I knew he was trying to make me laugh. It worked. My first real laughs in a long time.

My mother's argument with my father must've been pretty bad. We didn't hear a peep from her that night, and she didn't come downstairs until morning.

"Chase?" she said, walking into the living room and finding him asleep on the sofa. There went my plan of having Chase up and in the kitchen eating so no one knew he'd stayed overnight.

I ran up the hall from the kitchen. "Shh... Mom."

My mother eyed me up and down. "What is he doing here?"

"His parents are out of town. He said there were some suspicious-looking people on their street."

She crossed her arms. "You're telling me he was afraid?"

"He's fifteen—still a kid, Mom. A tall kid, but still a kid."

Elle came into the room and looked at our mother, who was glaring at me. She took her hand. "Mom, french toast," she said, pulling her toward the kitchen and winking at me.

Nice save, Elle.

"You cooked?" asked my mother.

But we didn't make it out of the living room. Our front door flung open, and my father fell inside and onto the floor.

My mother screamed. Chase jumped up from the sofa. I yelled out, and we all ran to my father.

His face was bloody and bruised. His left arm bent in the wrong direction. His eyelids flickered and he let out a groan, barely conscious.

"Dad!" I grabbed his hand. "Call 911!"

My mother was on the phone in seconds.

"What happened?" I asked, still gripping his hand.

For a moment, my father's eyes opened slightly.

"R-r-r," he said. "R-aw."

"Raw. He's saying Raul," said Chase.

"Raul?" asked my mom.

"R-r-r—"

"Where, Dad? Where?" I shouted.

He mumbled something. My mother was shaking. I think she thought he was going to die right there. *I* thought he was going to die right there.

"He's in shock," said Chase.

I ran to the window, opened the blinds, and looked out to the street. A silver Honda was parked on the other side of the road. The silhouette of a driver was visible in the window. He looked at me and pulled away.

"What are we going to do?" asked Elle, wringing her hands. Tears ran down her babyish cheeks.

"Yes," Chase said into the phone. He'd taken it from my mother. "We need an ambulance. He was assaulted. 27851 Winchester. Yes. Hurry."

My mother pulled a bloodied piece of yellow paper from inside my father's jacket. "What is this?"

She read it aloud. "*Give me my money*. What does that mean?"

Chase and I looked at each other, not wanting to say anything. My father's eyes were closed, but he was breathing. Each breath was labored and slow. He had to be in a lot of pain.

"Dad?" said Elle.

"Dad, how did you get home?" I asked. I lowered my ear down to him.

"They let me go," he said, spitting out a mouthful of blood. "Took me somewhere. Said they had my kids. Was a trick. A trick."

"They dropped you off?" I asked.

He described what happened in broken sentences. He'd been attacked by five thugs. They were after money, he said. But he didn't know why. I looked at Chase, who was still holding the phone, I knew he was thinking the same thing I was.

An ambulance and two police cruisers pulled up in front of our house, loudly calling attention to the whole street. Neighbors stopped walking their dogs, some came outside in pajamas and robes holding up their phones to film, and some stopped in the street just short of our yard so they could hear everything or perhaps ask questions.

We told the officers only what we'd seen, and my mother insisted we leave out the part about the note.

"Trust me," she said. "I'll explain later."

I nodded, not letting on that I knew anything about his money problems.

As the paramedics put my father on a stretcher, a muscle-bound officer bounded up our front steps, calling my name.

"Officer Spencer?" I replied.

"I heard the call," he said, looking around the living room. "Is everyone okay?"

"My dad," I replied, pointing at the stretcher.

He watched the paramedics and followed the other officers. They spoke quietly for a moment before he came back over to me and Chase.

My mother didn't speak. She held her fist, stained with my father's blood, over her mouth.

Officer Spencer glanced at her. He took a notepad from his pocket, grabbed a pen from the side table, and wrote fast. He tore off the paper and handed it to my mother. "That's my number. Call me. We need to talk."

About fifteen minutes later, the ambulance and police were gone. Officer Spencer left with the ambulance and my mother, and Chase and I stayed with Elle.

"What are we going to do?" I asked. "They could've killed my father."

Chase looked up and down the street, then shut the front door. "Are you sure it was Raul? I mean, your father's addiction is on a crazy level—like out of control—and he could owe a lot of people."

He looked up, noticing I hadn't responded.

I stormed out of the room toward the kitchen.

"What did I say?" he asked Elle. "What did I say?"

"You don't know when to shut up," she replied.

They joined me in the kitchen, where Elle's french toast sat on the counter, growing cold.

Chase picked up a slice and bit into it. After swallowing, he glanced at me and said, "I'm sorry. I kind of saw you as me, on the outside looking in, trying to solve a mystery. Not related to the victim. Scratch that. I don't know what I'm saying. I'm sorry."

"What are we going to do?" I asked again. "I even stood in front of the hall mirror, but Micah didn't appear."

Chase swallowed another bite. "Raul wants his money or you. One way or the other."

"Then give him his friggin' money."

Elle pushed her hands in front of her. "You have it?"

Elle wiped tears from her eyes. "My dad got beaten up for nothing? You have the money? Why wouldn't you just give it to that monster?"

Chase finished his toast and leaned his elbows on the counter. "It's not that simple, Elle."

She clapped her hands three times and leaned toward Chase. "Could you break it down for me then, Mister hacker teenager? Bad guy wants money. We have money. We don't give it to bad guy. Bad guy beats up father. Something is very wrong with this picture."

Chase grabbed his jacket from the back of the kitchen chair he'd sat in earlier and put it on.

"Where are you going?" I asked.

"Elle is right. I could've prevented this. Here, Brie. Hold on to this." He handed me the manilla envelopes.

I took them, frowning. "Why aren't you taking the money with you?"

"To make sure they are going to do what they say." Chase paused and held out his hand. "Actually, give me one of them. I will give Raul the rest after he assures me Mr. London's debt is cleared and you guys will never see his goons again."

I handed him the envelope. "I'm going with you."

He tucked it into his jacket and zipped it. "No, you're not. They want to kidnap you, remember?"

"How do you know where to go?" I asked.

"Raul owns the Oak Room. It's not just a club, it's his office. His hangout."

"And you're just going to walk in there? Your plan is very amateurish," said Elle.

Chase sighed and ran a hand over his dreads. "Well, it's all I've got."

After Chase left, I ran up the stairs to my room with my own plan. A half-hour later, I came downstairs wearing jeans, a baseball cap, and a black hoodie with the hood pulled over my head. Looking at my reflection in the hallway mirror, I thought I looked just like a typical teen boy. You can call me hardheaded if you want. I wouldn't argue with you. But Micah sure didn't show up in the mirror to tell me I was making a mistake or to stay put.

"Be careful," Elle said from behind me. She wrapped her arms around my waist and squeezed me tight.

I turned and hugged her back, inhaling the coconut scent of her hair. I needed to remember this moment if I made it home safely and our lives went back to normal. When Elle refused to leave my room or used my things or kicked at my door, this memory might keep me from trying to duct tape her to the hammock chair hanging from the ceiling in the corner of her bedroom.

She sniffed. "You're not going to go inside his hangout right, Brie? Just wait outside. Promise?"

"Promise," I replied. We'd looked up the directions and used the street view map to find the exact location of the Oak Room and noted the back alley. "Keep the doors locked and turn on the alarm. If someone breaks in, don't—"

"I know, I know. Don't hide under the bed or inside the closet. Keep the grill lighter fluid with me and set the house on fire."

I gasped. "Elle!"

She smiled weakly. "Okay, that was a bad joke. We have that cabinet in the kitchen that Dad cleared out. I can fit in there."

After I let go of her, she grabbed a hammer from the side table. She must have brought it in from Dad's tool shed to use as a weapon if need be.

I snuck out the back door, bent low so I couldn't be seen over the fence, and took the bus downtown. The alley behind the Oak Room was just as we'd seen on the street view of the map app. It smelled like urine and spoiled food.

The back door of the nearest four-story building opened, and I jumped beside a dumpster. A man and woman walked away in the opposite direction. From their conversation, I gathered they were just getting off work and in the mood for steak.

I waited with my back against the dumpster and flipped over the pepper spray in my pocket, afraid I'd have to actually use it. You only have seconds to get it right. What if I turned it in the wrong direction and sprayed it into my own eyes?

The problem with my plan was I didn't know which door Chase went in or would come out of. *Should I go inside or stay hidden?* It just didn't feel right—him going in there by himself.

The back door opened again, and a man came out and walked right past me. He walked with a hurried limp, like he was trying to escape something, and didn't notice me.

Moments later, the back door reopened. I peeked around the dumpster. Two stocky men tossed someone out onto the ground.

My heart pounded as I waited until the men went back inside, then I ran over to the man they'd tossed out. A familiar face blinked up at me. "Chase!"

"What are you doing here?" he asked, dazed.

I leaned over him, grasping his shoulders. "Chase, you have a black eye. Come on, we have to get out of here."

He put his arm around my shoulder, and I helped him up. With him leaning on me for balance, we walked toward the end of the alley.

The building door squealed open behind us.

"You didn't account for the cameras, did you?" asked Chase.

"Cameras?" Why didn't I think of that? "Come on, hurry!"

He clung to me as I tried to drag him faster.

A car pulled up in front of us, and we stopped. *The silver Honda. The same one I saw outside my house that sped off. They're boxing us in.* I looked over my shoulder. The two men in black suits stood outside the back door. One of them pointed at us.

The passenger window of the Honda rolled down. The driver was wearing a white mask with holes in it.

"Get in!" he barked.

"Who are you?" I demanded.

"We'll talk about that later. Right now, you need to get in!"

"You're wearing a freaking hockey mask! We're not getting in there."

Footsteps sounded behind us.

"Gabby, get your butt in here!" the driver shouted.

He called me Gabby. Like Micah. I don't know why I did it, but I opened the back seat door and pushed Chase inside, then squeezed practically on top of him. Hockey Face pulled off before I could close the door.

The tires squealed against the road, the sound shrill enough to wake the dead, as we wove through traffic. We sped, skidding around street corners. I screamed as we ran red light after red light. Horns beeped at us, and cars braked in the nick of time before they could collide with us.

Hockey Face finally slowed the car as we approached a parking garage. He drove through it and exited on the opposite side. We pulled up to a storage facility, and he hit the button on his key fob, which opened the gate. It closed behind us, and we pulled up to a storage unit. The driver used the fob again to raise the storage door, then he pulled inside.

Chase and I got out of the back seat. I looked around at the roomy garage. It had a leather loveseat, a cot with a pillow and blanket, and a desk with several computer monitors.

"Do you live here?" I asked.

He held a finger to his masked lip, then sat at the desk and turned on the computer. The screens showed images of the exterior of the building and the main gate.

"Clear," he said.

"Who are you?" asked Chase. "Why did you help us?"

"And why were you outside of my house?" I added.

Chase gave me a wide-eyed look. "He was? When?"

"Yes. When my dad came in, beaten."

Chase stormed over to the man, grabbed him, and spun him around in his chair.

"Dude, you don't want to do that," the man said with a British accent. He shoved Chase's hand from his shoulder and lowered his mask.

My chest hitched. "I know you. Hey, you were at Micah's funeral."

"I didn't see him there," said Chase.

But I was sure. Hockey Face now wore the same gray hoodie and torn jeans he'd worn at the funeral.

"Yeah, he was there," I said. "He stood off at a distance, watching everything."

Hockey Face got up from his chair and wandered to the mini-fridge next to the couch. "I've been trying to get to you ever since. It shouldn't have been this hard or taken this long," he said as he took out a package of ice. He handed it to Chase. "For your face. This guy went to see Raul for some stupid reason. You could've gotten yourself killed. Dumb move, guy."

Chase held the ice to his eye, wincing. "It was dumb all right. That wasn't even half the money."

"What?" I asked, still holding my pepper spray.

Chase groaned. "Yep, he took the envelope I had, but he wants all of it, so where's the rest?"

"Why are you talking about this in front of him? We don't know him," I said, holding my pepper spray pointed at Hockey Face.

"He's Shaun," said Chase. "You're Shaun, right?"

Hockey Face nodded, setting his mask on top of the fridge. "Yeah."

"And you live in a storage unit?" I asked.

He shrugged. "I'm off the grid."

"You helped Micah get the money, didn't you? So where is it?" I demanded.

"There's more to this than money," said Shaun. "That's why I've been trying to get to you before this whole thing explodes. Micah and I started digging, and once you start digging, you're bound to unearth something rotten. We found out everything Raul is mixed up in." He reached into the fridge, then tossed me a bottled water. "Your father and Raul, they used to be friends. Back when your dad's account was in good standing."

He went to the computer and tapped on the keyboards as he spoke, then hopped into the desk chair. "Look, I did what Micah paid me to do, and I tried to stay out of it. But something wasn't right. The way he fell sick as soon as all of this happened..." He shook his head.

I bit my lip. "You're saying someone made him sick."

"Illness would be an easy way to get rid of someone without leaving a trail. No one would think murder."

Even with a bruised eye, I could see Chase's I-told-you-so expression. "So where is the rest of the money?" he asked.

"That's between you and him," Shaun said. "If Micah only made some of it available, I'm assuming he knew someone would know where to find the rest. Someone who knew him well."

Chase and I looked at each other.

"Her. I meant her," said Shaun, pointing at me.

"I have no idea where it is." I looked around the storage room, then walked over to a cabinet in the corner and opened it.

"Hey!" said Shaun. "Do you know what privacy is? Those are my clothes."

Besides his clothes, which were all gray or black, a mirror hung on the door.

"Can you close that?" asked Shaun.

I stood there, staring at the mirror. Micah's reflection looked back at me, and my breath caught.

"What's wrong with her?"

Chase walked over and stood behind me. He inhaled sharply, clearly seeing Micah too.

Shaun groaned. "Great. Now it's both of them over there staring into the underverse or something. Seriously, can you both stop it? You're freaking me out." He joined us, scowling. "What are you—"

He looked at the mirror, then collapsed, but Chase caught him before he could hit the floor.

I gasped. "Is he breathing?"

"Yes." Chase lightly smacked his jaw. "Shaun!"

He straightened as if startled out of his sleep, pulling away from Chase. He turned toward the mirror. "Did I just see—was that Micah?"

Chase nodded. "Yes, and he's trying to tell us something."

Shaun looked at the mirror again, but Micah was gone. What looked like a layer of tiny snowflakes coated the reflective surface.

Where did that come from? "Shaun, what were you doing around the Oak Room?" I asked.

"Yeah, how did you happen to be there?" said Chase.

"I followed you." He kept his gaze on the mirror. He pointed at it. "That's not right."

"Yeah, we know, tell us about it," Chase said, plopping onto the sofa in the middle of the room.

"But it's happening," I added, taking a seat beside him. "We saw Micah in that reflection too."

Shaun walked over to us. "So did he just look at you, or did he tell you something?"

"I don't know," I replied. "We were too busy dealing with your reaction to him."

Shaun walked up and down the only clear path of the storage unit, rubbing his chin. "School locker?"

Chase scrunched his nose. "What?"

Shaun snapped his fingers. "The money. Stay focused will ya?"

"I emptied his hall and gym lockers for his parents," said Chase. "There was no money."

I stood and picked up a photo from his desk, frowning at the familiar girl in it. "How do you know Ashlyn?"

"He knows Ashlyn?" Chase took the photo from me and looked it over.

"She's my girl," said Shaun.

"Do you know she's looking for you?" I replied. "She's distraught and doesn't know where you are."

"Oh, that's because we had an argument. I move around a lot. You tell her where I am. Now, back on the subject. Could the money be in your locker?" he asked, pointing at me.

I shook my head. "No. I mean, there's not much in there, but I don't think so."

Shaun wagged his finger. "Micah kept talking about winter break…"

I glanced at the cabinet. "Winter … Oh my gosh, the mirror crystalized."

"When?" Shaun demanded.

"After you fainted. You just saw it. It looked like snowflakes. That was a clue."

"The road trip?" asked Chase.

"Where were you guys going?" Shaun asked.

"I'm not sure he'd want you to know this. I mean it's not very—" I scratched my head. "You know, stuff guys do."

Chase crossed his arms. "I really don't think his reputation is at stake right now."

"The M&M factory. He went there last winter break too."

"In New York City or Vegas?" asked Shaun.

"New York. And how do you know where the factories are, Shaun?" I asked.

"Man, he was obsessed with M&Ms," said Chase.

Shaun pointed at me. "None of your business. And you," he said, knocking Chase's feet off the table. "Keep your feet on the floor."

Chase scowled at him, then righted his seat. "So we have to go to the M&M factory in New York, then?"

I shook my head. "Think about it, that's a three-hour drive. When would Micah have time to go there to hide the money? He would've had to take the train, but he had a job. No, he couldn't have done that."

"Unless someone did it for him... Or," Shaun clapped his hands and pointed at me. "It's only a clue."

"M&Ms are just a clue?" I thought for a moment and stood. "I know where he hid the money. We can end this tonight."

Shaun wiped his hands together. "Okay, well, my work is done. You don't know me. You never saw me. If you come back here tomorrow, you'll find the storage unit cleared out."

I put my hands on my hips. "But how can you do that?"

"Oh, my dad owns a lot of these storage facilities."

"Then how will Ashlyn find you?" I asked.

He shrugged. "Just tell her to come here. Don't worry, she'll find me."

"But you're a tattoo artist," said Chase.

"Only when I want to be. And then, like a puff of vapor, I disappear." Shaun wiggled his fingers in the air.

I groaned. "Stop being so dramatic. Are you going to give us a ride or not?"

Shaun went to his car and peeled at the paint on the door. "As soon as you help me remove this wrap."

Shaun's car was red now, and I wondered if that coat was another wrap that could be peeled off too. I got the feeling he really thought he was a member of MI6.

I sat in the passenger seat as we sped down the street. "I bet you watch a lot of James Bond movies," I said to Shaun.

He grinned, gripping the steering wheel. "I do. But like I said, I don't watch them for the car chases, I watch for the romance. I'm a lover and a hacker, not a fighter."

"You sure drive like it," Chase grumbled from the back seat.

Shaun ignored him, rubbing his chin. "I think I'm more of a *Mission Impossible* man."

We pulled up to our destination.

"There," I said, pointing at the store.

Shaun frowned as he parked the car. "I thought this was a corner market. It's a bodega."

"It's where Micah worked," I replied.

Viny plants hung from the fire escape above the entrance of the brick building. Graffiti stood out on the side of the building that read, "Eminem was here."

I glanced at Chase in the back seat. "Chase, look, the clue. Eminem. M&M. Get it?"

"Hmm..." He furrowed his brows. "Maybe."

The lights shone through the front windows of the building, and I thought I saw movement inside. I looked at Chase again. "I think it's open."

"Did you think it would be closed?" he replied. "How the heck would we get inside? They lock this place down like Fort Knox."

Shaun let out an exasperated sigh. "Don't argue in my car. Get out. And I mean that in the nicest way."

I unbuckled my seatbelt and hopped out of the car. Chase joined me on the sidewalk.

I leaned over and looked in the unrolled window. "Thanks, Shaun."

He scrubbed his face with his hand. "Er—Shaun isn't really my name, so you can stop calling me that. And now, I will disappear into the wind," he said with a grin as he pulled away.

He's so weird. But I liked him.

We watched the red Honda until it turned a corner, then I looked at the shop. *What if I got it wrong? What if this was not what Micah was trying to tell us?*

We approached the store, and Micah's reflection appeared in the window next to the poster of various sandwiches and below the lottery sign. *I guess I'm not wrong.*

"Okay, he's here. I think that's a sign," said Chase.

We walked inside. A woman stood at the counter, which was framed in cubbies containing all types of candies, nuts, and gum. Chase followed me down an aisle.

"Where are you going?" he whispered. "Should I sneak into the back?"

I shook my head, pretending to browse. "You have a black eye. You look suspicious. Just stay with me."

The M&Ms were our first stop. They were in an aisle with large bags of potato chips, pretzels, and popcorn. The cartons of candy bars were all king-sized. Chase grabbed all the M&M bags from the shelf and looked behind them, running his hand behind the other items. His hand came out covered in dust.

He wiped it on his pant leg. "It's not here."

"I know it's in this store, we just have to find it. You were Micah's best friend. Think like him."

"Okay," Chase whispered. "I get to work before everyone else, and I have to hide a bag of money quickly. In a place that weeks later, no one will have found." He thought for a moment. "The ceiling?"

I crossed my arms, thinking. "I don't think so. It would be too hard to get to."

We walked down the aisle of canned goods and condiments.

"Don't you have a mirror?" Chase asked, peering closely at a shelf filled with hygiene products. "Micah could point it out to us or something."

I held my arms out to the sides "Do you not see I'm dressed like a boy? I don't have a purse. And stop looking over there. He wouldn't have hidden it near dandruff shampoos and feminine products."

The woman at the counter craned her neck, watching us.

"I think she's going to call the cops," Chase said. "You have to move."

"Why would she call the cops on me?" I hissed. "I'm not doing anything wrong."

"Yes, you are. You're just standing in the middle of the aisle, looking suspicious."

"So are you." I elbowed him. "Pick up something." I picked up a can and inspected the label, then thrust it into his hand. "Here, take these canned weenie things to the counter. Distract her while I look."

It was a small place, but quite a few customers milled around, some ordering deli sandwiches, others shopping or scratching instant lottery tickets.

"Sal! Salvador! Give me that ham and cheese," a man yelled with a hand in the air. "Don't front. You know how I like it. Make it crispy, Sal. Burn the edges a little."

A display filled with bags of Cheetos sat at the end of the aisle. It hung from the end of the top shelf almost to the floor, and a cooler stood nearby. I looked around the cooler and up the aisle.

Chase returned to my side after asking the clerk about the canned weenies. A popping noise went off like someone had stuck a needle in a balloon. Chase and I looked in the direction it came from. M&Ms were dropping to the floor from their shelf like confetti. Red, orange, yellow, and brown candies rolled toward us.

"The floor is uneven," Chase whispered.

The M&Ms stopped at the cooler.

I raised a brow. "How did that happen?"

Chase shook his head. "We should pick them up," he said as he knelt. "Someone might slip on one."

As I helped him scoop up the candies, I noticed something different about the wall directly behind the cooler. A strip of the base was black instead of white. As I got closer, I saw it wasn't even the same texture as the wall.

"Look!" I nudged Chase, pointing at the section.

"Is that it?" he asked, dropping his handful of candy.

I nodded. "I think so. It's wedged inside like someone carved the drywall out."

Chase tried pulling at it. "It's in there tight."

"Get out of the way," I said. "Let me try. My hands are smaller. I can dig it out."

Chase straightened and stepped aside.

I grabbed the cooler door for leverage and pulled on the baseboard section until it opened wide. Chase pretended to look in the cooler at yogurt flavors. Micah's reflection watched me from the cooler door.

The board wouldn't budge anymore, so I placed a foot on the wall for leverage.

"What are you doing? You're going to hurt yourself," said Chase.

"It's stuck."

Back and forth, back and forth, I had to work it as I pulled. Finally, I smiled and looked up at Chase. "We did it."

I peered into the dark hole and almost didn't see the rectangular black bag. The way it was positioned, it looked like part of the wall. I grabbed it, my heart racing. It was about three inches thick. The size of a few stacks of bills.

My phone vibrated, scaring me, and I dropped the bag. Chase quickly picked it up.

I pulled out my phone and read my messages.

Elle: Are you okay or not?

Me: Yes, I'm okay, we found the money.

Elle: Where?

Me: Micah's workplace.

Chase glanced at my phone and shot me a look.

"What?" I asked. "If I don't tell her she'll keep harassing us."

Elle: Good, Mom called. And there's a car outside.

Me: Okay. Remember what I said. I'm on my way.

Elle: Right. Burn down the house. Got it.

I shook my head, shoving my phone back inside my pocket.

"We don't have time for texting. Let's go," said Chase.

"You're not going anywhere," said a voice from behind us. "Give me that."

How did we not notice someone was watching us? The man tugged at his apron and held out his hand for the bag, his cheeks and nose reddening. I recognized him as Micah's old boss, Mr. Vega.

"You're so bad at this," I told Chase.

"Me? You're the one who—"

Mr. Vega growled. "Did you hear what I said?"

I gave him my best smile. "Mr. Vega, you know me. It's Brie. Micah's girlfriend."

He narrowed his eyes at me. "Oh, is that you, Brie?"

"Yes."

Mr. Vega never showed evidence of having problems with his sight before, so I was surprised he acted like he hadn't recognized me.

"He was being sarcastic," said Chase.

I swallowed. "Oh."

The man reached his hand toward me with his palm up. "In case you didn't know, whatever you find in this store belongs to me."

Chase took a step back, clutching the bag. "No."

"What do you mean, no?"

"It doesn't belong to you," I said. "This was Micah's. He left it for me."

Mr. Vega raised a brow. "If it was yours, he wouldn't have left it in this store."

Chase scowled, handing me the bag. "You don't know what you're talking about."

"I've been watching you from the time you walked in the door, through that mirror on the ceiling." He grabbed the bag with a wrinkled hand, trying to pull it away from me.

"Let go!" I yanked the bag, digging my fingers into its sides.

"This doesn't have to get nasty," said a deep voice behind Mr. Vega. "Let go of the bag."

The hockey-masked person held a pistol at Mr. Vega's back, and the store owner let go of the bag and raised his arms.

"Scram," he told us. Then he held up the pistol, showing us it was really a soda bottle.

Chase and I ran outside, and we were greeted by a police car pulling up in front of us, blocking off the corner of the alley.

"The other way!" yelled Chase.

We turned to run.

The cop got out of the car. "Gabby!"

"It's Officer Spencer!" I stopped and turned to face him.

"Brie, you don't stop just because someone calls your name," said Chase, who had stopped a few feet ahead of me. "Remind me to never go on the run with you."

Shaun ran up behind us from the store, holding his hockey mask and the bottle.

I gaped at him. "You came back for us."

"I never left. You two are not cut out for this." He shook his head. "I had to see it through."

"Who called the police?" asked Chase.

"Gabby's sister," said Officer Spencer.

"Elle." I'd forgotten Officer Spencer had left his number at my house. "She was worried about us."

"Come with me," said Officer Spencer, just as Mr. Vega ran outside.

He huffed, pointing at us. "I'm glad you're here, Officer. Arrest them. That's my property she has."

I gripped the bag tighter. "No, it's not. It's Micah's. He's trying to take it from me."

"She's telling the truth," said Chase.

"Exactly what's in the bag, sir?" asked Officer Spencer.

"Uh, my stuff," said Mr. Vega.

"Your stuff, huh?" Officer Spencer raised a skeptical brow. "Clothes, food, what?"

Mr. Vega rubbed his head. "I can't remember."

Officer Spencer crossed his arms in an authoritative stance. "Well then, this bag is going to the station, and I think you better go back inside and wait for me before I arrest you for assaulting a minor."

"I'll see you in court," Mr. Vega yelled, glaring at me.

I shot him a smirk. "Can't wait."

Mr. Vega stormed back into the store.

"Is that legal?" I asked Officer Spencer. "Can you just send him away like that?"

Officer Spencer nodded. "It will hold him while you tell me what is really going on."

Chase and I looked at each other.

"Unless you want to go downtown?" Officer Spencer looked around. "What happened to that kid who was just here?"

I glanced behind me. There was no sign of Shaun anywhere.

We unzipped the bag and showed Officer Spencer the bills inside it.

He pushed back his hat, his eyes wide. "You've got to be kidding. Why did Micah have that?"

"It wasn't really his," Chase replied. "It belongs to Raul."

Officer Spencer frowned. "You mean Raul Whitman. Raul from—"

Chase nodded. "Yes, that Raul."

Officer Spencer straightened. "Micah was a good kid. Why would he be mixed up with Raul?"

Chase and I glanced at each other.

"Look, I'm tired of you looking at each other," Officer Spencer said, waving his hand between us.

"Tell me what the heck is going on, and don't leave anything out."

So we told him the whole story, as incredulous as it was.

When we were done, Officer Spencer looked away from us, staring at the brick wall of the building, as if trying to work out a puzzle in his head.

"Do you believe us?" I asked.

He swallowed, glancing at me. "I-I'm going to have to. But this is not a story I can take back to the station. I'm going to need evidence. I have an idea, and hopefully this will get Raul off your father's back."

I sighed in relief.

Officer Spencer nodded at his car. "Oh, and I sent a car to your sister, so don't worry about her."

Chase raised a hand. "Are you sure they aren't on Raul's payroll? Because—"

"This is not one of those bad cop movies." Officer Spencer turned away and pulled out his phone.

"I can't believe I'm back here," said Chase, gazing at the front door of the Oak Room. The beat of the music blasted from inside.

"Hopefully for the last time," I replied.

Chase pulled me through the cigarette smoke, past all the people waiting, to the front of the line. "We want to see Raul," he told the bouncer.

The bouncer grunted. "I don't know a Raul. But if you want to get in here, you're going to have to show me some ID."

Chase pulled me in front of him and snatched off my cap and hood. My hair fell from beneath it, and the bouncer looked me over.

"Yo, watch the door," he told the thick-necked bruiser behind him, then he opened the door and stepped inside the club.

We waited while the hulk stared down at us.

After a few minutes, the first bouncer returned and nodded at the other. "Let them through."

The hulk didn't move, so we squeezed along the side of him and followed the first bouncer into the club.

"Sheesh, do they know they hired a wall?" said Chase.

On the other side of the door was a world like nothing I'd ever seen. Why would I have? I was only fifteen.

The club was filled with all types of people. Men wore suits. Women in tight dresses. Old people, young people, all sitting at tables with drinks or dancing on the dance floor.

There were people everywhere, making it hard to get around. The Oak Room may not have been the only club in town, but it had to be the most popular. The two-story club was much bigger than I'd expected, with an upstairs lounge and a dance floor downstairs.

I scanned the room and spotted a red sign that said PLEASE KEEP SHOES ON. In front of the sign was a large stage that extended to the middle of the dance floor, and a DJ booth at the side.

The bouncer led us through the mass of people, and we were stopped by another man who was built like a tank.

I looked up at him. He was much bigger than the hulk at the door. He said something in the other's ear.

"Wait here," the first bouncer yelled, leaving us near the bar.

Chase banged his fist on the counter. "I want a beer."

The spiky-haired bartender took one look at Chase, and then at me, and laughed.

"If you're eighteen, I'll buy you a beer," he told Chase.

Chase frowned and shrugged him off.

The bouncer came back and waved his hand for us to follow him.

As we walked, I took everything in. The atmosphere. The people I tried not to bump into. The energy. The music, loud and fast. Something didn't sit right with me. The place felt dark. My gut churned with unease.

And then I saw Raul.

He sat on a couch, surrounded by people, laughing and holding a wine glass. He didn't see us at first. Chase and I made a beeline for him.

Everyone turned and stared at us. They were probably wondering what a couple of kids were doing in a place like this flanked by giants.

"Raul!" Chase exclaimed.

Raul looked our way, set his wine glass on the table in front of him, then stood and adjusted his suit jacket. His presence made me take a step back.

The people beside him moved aside as if cued to get lost.

"What are you doing here?" he asked Chase. "Can I help you?"

"You can." Chase walked up to him. "You don't recognize me? How about the bruises on my face?"

Raul looked at me. I suddenly had the impulse to turn and run back the way we'd come. He took a step toward me, and my throat tightened. His attractiveness didn't make the encounter any less frightening. His deep-set, dark brown eyes and dark hair complimented his tan skin. He was tall, muscular, and had a very intimidating presence.

My heart raced wildly inside my chest. I wasn't prepared for a physical altercation. In my head, I quickly went over all the things I'd learned about self-defense in school. Did I still have my pepper spray? Would it even work on a human rottweiler?

He motioned with his head, and the bouncers pushed us through a doorway and into another room. They closed the door behind us.

"So this is Gabriella." Raul stepped into my space. He lifted my chin, turned it left and right, and then turned his attention back to Chase. "You saved us the trouble of coming for her. I appreciate that."

I recoiled from him. "No. I-I'm here to ask you to leave my father alone. You didn't have to hurt him."

"Your father is a grown man. And he knows there are consequences to his actions." Raul waved a finger. "The problem is, Lorenzo has no self-control. It's a disease, you know? Gambling."

"We can make a deal right now," said Chase. "You leave her father alone, and no one will know that you killed a girl."

My stomach clenched. *Why did he say that? He wasn't supposed to say that.*

Chase had tried to sound confident. But his face gave him away. He looked worried. Scared.

"I'm sorry, what?" asked Raul. "What girl?"

"The girl that's missing. Emily," Chase replied. "Yeah, we know about her. You're a killer."

Raul looked around at the other men in the room. "You're going to have to be a little more specific about who you mean. In this room, there are many killers."

The words sent chills up my spine. He openly admitted to his horrible acts!

Raul pointed at Chase. "I think it's time for you to go. But she's staying with me," he said, motioning toward me.

"I'm not going anywhere." Chase scowled, puffing his chest. "You kill someone, and then you play it off like it's fine. Like you're innocent. Like a life doesn't matter. I have evidence, and if you end all of this gangster stuff, I won't give it to the police."

Raul looked to the side and then nodded. He walked away, and his henchmen pushed us along after him. He led us to another door and unlocked it. "What girl? You mean this girl?"

He swung open the door, and I peered into the dark room. I heard a cry, and then the missing girl ran out screaming. Emily looked scared beyond anything I had ever seen. One of the guards caught her over his arm, and she kicked and punched at him. She was dirty and wild.

"What did you do to her?" I asked.

"Right now, nothing. We've been waiting for payment. She mostly screams, bites, and scratches." Raul rubbed his chin, smirking. "But all lions can be tamed."

"Lunatic! She's autistic!" Chase shouted.

The bouncer shoved Emily back inside the room and slammed the door.

Raul shrugged. "I don't care if she's artsy."

"You can't be that stup—" I took a deep breath. "Autistic, not artistic. Autism Spectrum Disorder. She's used to a certain routine, people, and environment. Changes to those can freak her out."

Raul gritted his teeth. "Whatever. Do. You. Have. My. Money? Last chance, before I put you in there with your autistic friend."

"I have it," said Chase. "Just let them both go."

"No," I said. "Chase, you can't pay these people, and you can't stop them. We were wrong. We need to get out of here."

Raul sneered. "That sounds about right, but you should have thought about that before you came here."

Raul reached for me, and Chase charged at him. He tried to slug the gangster, but the guards were on him before he could get in a punch. They slammed him to the cement floor. He kicked at Raul a few times, but they heaved him to his feet and dragged him away from the man.

"Don't hurt him!" I exclaimed. I ran to Chase, pulling at his legs. They pulled him out of my grasp, and one of the guards yanked me back and pushed me toward Raul.

Raul turned to me, reaching for my neck.

"I have it," Chase yelled. "I have your money!"

Raul stopped and lowered his hand. "Well?"

Chase tried to jerk free of the bouncers. "I need my hands to get to it."

They let Chase go, and he reached for the bag. The tape that had been holding it to his skin beneath his shirt ripped off, and he grimaced.

Raul lifted a hand toward him. "He's wearing the money? Didn't anyone pat him down?"

"Here." Chase tossed the bag to the bouncer beside him.

Raul waited as the bouncer opened the bag and nodded at him. "And where is the information you have on me, and don't lie. I know you do."

Chase tossed him the USB drive.

I ran to the door that held Emily and opened it. Giving her a comforting look, I held my hand out to her. "Come, let's go."

"That's to free you, not her," said Raul.

"It's a two-for-one," said Chase.

Raul opened his jacket, revealing a pistol. "Only one of them will leave here with you tonight."

"Don't you put your hands on her," Chase said.

The guards were heading for him again.

Emily gave me a desperate look, and I squeezed her hand. "I'll stay," I yelled.

"No, you won't," said Chase.

I looked at him and pulled Emily out of the dim room. "I won't leave her here. Look at her."

"Looks like we're finished here," said Raul.

Chase ran over to us and touched Emily's arm. "Emily, are you okay? I'm going to take you home."

"Home," Emily said, nodding. She shivered, and I wasn't sure if it was from being cold or afraid. "Take me home, Gabby."

"How did you know my name?" I asked.

"My name is Emily."

"I know."

"Emily London Fulton." She pointed at the faint outline of a mirror on the wall in the room she'd been kept in. "Micah told me you would come."

Emily took my hand, and I led her toward the door to the club area. She stayed behind me with her eyes lowered.

Raul sneered after us. "Look at you—already getting along. I knew this would work out. You know, it's your father you should be upset with, not me. He's the one who got you into all of this."

"I was upset with him at first," I said. "But if you have the power to hold a grudge, then you have the power to forgive. Forgiveness is a choice."

Raul clapped his hands as if I'd just given a performance.

"You better hope God forgives you for all you've done," Chase told him.

Raul narrowed his eyes at Chase. "You think God cares about you? You think God is watching over you and your black eye? If he was, why would you be here right now? God doesn't have any part in this. I built this." Raul slapped himself on the chest. "This is my world." He laughed. It was a perfectly good laugh gone bad, like a perfectly good egg gone bad, right down to the pungent smell and unbearable taste.

"Things change," I said. "Nothing is permanent."

Suddenly, screams rang out from the club area, followed by a loud crash and footsteps running toward us.

One of the bouncers stuck his head outside the door, then glanced over his shoulder at Raul. "It's the police."

Raul jerked his head toward the guard.

"I patted him down. He's clear," the man said.

"That's a lie. And look here." I held the charm up from my necklace. "Say cheese."

Raul's eyes widened.

The guards surrounded Raul and grabbed him, turning him to the back door. But at the same time, he grabbed me as the police came through the other side of the room with guns drawn.

"Police! Drop your weapons!" they shouted.

The guards fired at the police. Chase tackled Emily, and Raul kept running, dragging me with him.

Sirens came from every direction.

"Let go of me," I yelled, trying to jerk away from him.

Raul only grunted and breathed heavily, holding me tighter.

I bit his hand, twisted myself from his grip, and ran. Raul pounded after me and grabbed my hair, dragging me with him again.

"You're crazy!" I screamed, slapping at his hands. "You're going to go to jail."

He ignored me, still dragging me along until we were out on the street.

"Let me go!" I screamed.

He let go of my hair and shoved me. Hard.

I fell backward onto my butt and hit something hard with my head. I tasted blood on my tongue. Blood from biting my lip. I looked up to see what I'd hit. A fire hydrant.

Raul came closer to me, but I jumped up and pushed him away from me. I spotted an alleyway and rushed down it. Raul was so fast, he caught up and grabbed me again, pulling me to his chest as I tried to fight him off.

"You thought that was smart? It was stupid," he said and snatched the chain from my neck. He tossed it aside. "I'm going to teach you a lesson," he whispered, his warm breath hitting my skin. I swallowed hard, my heart pounding as he leaned in closer. "You want to know why?"

The blood drained from my face.

I guess he expected me to answer. I didn't. I just stared at him.

"Because I can," he hissed.

He slammed my back into the brick wall of the building next to us, and I struggled to breathe. I opened my mouth to scream, and he covered it with his hand. Terror like I'd never experienced before filled me.

He glared at me. "You have no idea who I am or what I'll do to you. And right now, you're my security."

He yanked my wrists and dragged me through the streets, dodging people and cars as we went.

"Let me go!" I yelled. I knew I couldn't fight him. He was too strong. And the few people on the street only watched. No one got involved.

Raul pushed me behind a car and forced me to crouch with him as police cars sped by. As he watched the cruisers, I glanced at the parked cars. Micah's image appeared on the closest one's side mirror. It moved from that vehicle to the next.

Follow you? That had to be what he meant. Why else would his image move away from me? But how did he expect me to get away from Raul?

I looked around the curb for something I could use for a weapon. This must've been the cleanest street ever. There were no bottles or stones or anything.

When Raul pulled me to standing, I kneed him in the groin and bolted away, running with all my might. *He won't fire. I know he won't. It will bring the police this way.*

And I was right. Raul didn't fire. I thought he would let me go and run in the opposite direction to go into hiding or something, but he didn't. I think that kick to the groin enraged him, because he charged after me, pumping his arms and still holding the pistol.

Micah's image switched from car mirror to car mirror, and then it vanished. I spun around, searching the cars around me. "Where? Where are you?"

I looked in a store window behind me, and he was there. I started running again, and he appeared in each window as I passed. Then, his image leapt onto a bus, and I crossed the street, following it to a high-rise office building where Micah appeared on the glass doors. I ran up the steps and pulled on the door handles, but they wouldn't open. The place was locked down for the night, and there weren't any security guards in sight.

Oh no! Why did you lead me here?

"Dead end, huh?" Raul's voice came from behind me. "There's nowhere to run. Let's go."

I slowly turned. Raul held his pistol, pointed at me.

"Don't shoot," I said as I walked toward him with my hands up. "Please."

He smirked. "I thought letting you go could be a good thing, but you've caused too much trouble."

He raised his pistol to my face.

He's really going to do it. Where are the police? I closed my eyes and saw Micah's face, smiling in the sunlight, eyes glowing. *I love you,* I thought. *I'll be with you soon.*

But Raul didn't shoot. I opened my eyes. Raul focused on something above me. His expression shrank from confident killer to terrified random guy holding a gun.

"How?" he asked, taking a few steps back. "You're dead. I made sure of it. I saw you!"

I looked over my shoulder. The building was covered in mirrored glass, and Micah's reflection stood in each pane.

"He's not dead," I said, lowering my hands.

Micah's reflections merged into one and grew taller and taller over the building.

Raul started firing wildly everywhere Micah's reflection reappeared. I dove into the shrubs as shattered glass descended upon the walkway.

Moments later, an eerie silence fell as the shots stopped. The crashing glass halted. Raul lay on his back, his eyes open with a look of shocked horror, his arms splayed out to the side. Cuts and gashes covered him; blood poured from the wounds. A large, jagged piece of mirrored glass twirled in the air over his chest like a spinning top.

My eyes stinging, I rose from my crouched position behind the shrubs and walked toward Raul's body. Suddenly, the glass shattered on Raul's chest. My hands shot to my face to protect my eyes. Raul lay there unmoving. I didn't know if he was still breathing, and I didn't care. His pistol lay on the pavement a few feet from his hand. I grabbed it and tucked it under my belt. The USB drive was on the ground. I picked that up too. It was how the police were able to listen in on everything.

At first, I didn't see Micah. Then he reappeared in one of the cracked panes of the building. I walked closer to him with tears in my eyes. "I know what you did now. You made a promise to my father. You stayed for me. You could've gone to heaven, but you stayed to protect me."

Micah grinned.

"And Emily. You knew about her. You helped us save her."

Sirens blared and tires screeched in the street. Car doors slammed and footsteps pounded behind me.

"Brie!" Chase ran up to me, followed by Officer Spencer.

Chase was about to say something more, but he stopped, looking at Micah's reflection.

Micah spoke, his voice shaky. "I stayed for you and for the truth. Look at Emily."

I had. She looked like me, like Chase had said.

"He was holding her hostage as he was going to do to you," Micah continued. "Anyone attached to your father was in danger."

I tilted my head. "Attached to my father?"

Micah nodded. "She's your half-sister. Your father's daughter."

Raul knew. Who else knew? Did my mom? Gabriella London. She tried to tell me. Emily London Fulton.

"Don't hate anyone. Don't blame anyone. You have a long life ahead of you, Gabby. You choose what to do with it." Micah looked off to the side. A bright light grew behind him.

"Why did you come to us in mirrors?" I asked.

"I'm just a reflection of what's on the inside of you," he said. "Gabby, you're in control of your life. You can beat anorexia."

I nodded and placed my hand on the window. Micah placed his there too. And for a moment, I felt him.

A tear rolled down my cheek.

"Don't cry, Gabby," he said softly. "We all have to go sometime."

"Says the guy who is already gone," I said, sniffling. As I spoke, Shaun's reflection appeared behind Micah.

I gasped.

Micah nodded. "Raul found him before he got to me. Tell everyone where to find his body."

"The storage unit," Chase whispered, answering the question in my head. Shaun was missing. They thought he had disappeared like he usually did. And if my assumption was right, he was in the trunk of the Honda.

Micah began to fade.

I reached for him again. "Micah, wait. I..."

"Take care of my Gabby," he told Chase. "Best buds—"

"Forever," Chase said with him, freely crying.

Micah looked past me. "Officer Spencer, thank you. For everything."

Officer Spencer didn't make a sound. But for a moment, a little boy appeared beside Micah, raised his hand in the air, and faded away. I couldn't put in words the sound that came from Officer Spencer, and I couldn't turn away from Micah.

In an instant, Shaun was gone, and then Micah. He disappeared into the light with a smile on his face and a piece of my heart.

"But I didn't get to say I love you," I whispered.

"You think I didn't know that?" Micah's voice surrounded me.

I nodded with tear filled eyes. "Every day, with every breath. I love you."

"I've always known."

"Don't go…"

One Month Later

I can't say that everything felt right again. I'm not even sure I know what that means. But I was happy Micah was where he was supposed to be—in heaven. I finally stopped beating myself up, asking why I hadn't noticed what was going on with my father. For the past two years, I had been so distracted with my own mental state and illness, I guess I'd shut out what was happening with my family.

At first, I racked my brain, trying to figure things out. I wondered if I could have done something. And I thought of my mother and how much she had endured. Alone.

My father wore a cast, and though bruised on the outside, he seemed healed on the inside. The worry and frown lines were gone from his face, and he laughed heartily again. Especially when he joked about my middle name coming from the song "Copacabana," which I had to Google because I had no idea why that was funny. It was evident where I got my bad jokes from.

Seated on our couch with Elle's feet on my lap, I pulled up the song on my phone and read the lyrics. I cringed. "Dad! Seriously?"

In the armchair across from me, he glanced up from his tablet. "What? Let me see."

I read the lyrics aloud.

He raised his brows. "Oh wow, I forgot how it ends. I meant the name, not the story. Bad joke. I'm so sorry."

"Oh my gosh, Dad," said Elle, shooting him a mean look. "Lola was Mom's mom."

My dad stared at the floor, shaking his head, and suddenly exclaimed, "Who wants pizza?"

"Good recovery." I got up and kissed him on the forehead. "But for the record, I won't tolerate anchovies. Not today. And maybe we can invite someone who kind of looks like me?" I asked, squinting as if he were about to yell my ear off.

"I think that's a good idea," my mom said, walking into the room.

To the surprise of my parents, I started therapy again on my own, and we made some progress. I'd stopped eating because I'd thought I was the reason my dad had left all those years ago—because of my weight. I had never thought I was enough, and I had used not eating as a way of gaining control over something in my life. I can admit that now. I attended the group sessions after school with the rest of the mourners. Chase joined us too.

Every day, I looked in the mirror and said, "I'm okay. Micah, I'm okay." And it was true. I could hear people's words again, instead of just the hum of them. Colors looked brighter, as if they'd gone dull for a while before.

I made new friends and got closer to the ones I already had. I was so afraid of losing myself, but I'd lost myself a long time ago. I had thought I knew what I wanted, but I'd been wrong. My thoughts had been so twisted. I'd had to get through the pain to see that. It wasn't easy. But it was worth it. Now, my future was looking a lot brighter. I was alive and thriving, in the land of the living.

After school one day, Chase walked into the coffee shop and sat across from me and Ashlyn. He lifted his hand at the barista. "Tasha, a chai—"

"I've got you. I know what you like," she replied with a wink.

"I think you've got an admirer," I teased.

Chase grinned and rubbed his hand over his short dreads while sneaking another look at her. His bronze complexion was as bright as I'd ever seen it, his cheeks flushed with a light sheen of sweat.

"Chase, are you blushing? You are." I laughed.

He ignored me and looked at Ashlyn. "Anyway, did Brie tell you everything?"

Ashlyn shook her head and pulled her red waves behind her and over one shoulder. "It's so hard to believe."

"It's true, though," Chase said, confirming what I had told her earlier.

"And you say Shaun went to the light also? To heaven?"

I nodded. "We just thought you should know. We couldn't just leave it as his body was found in a storage unit. You had to hear the whole story, as incredulous as it sounds," I told her. "Shaun was— I don't know. He didn't tell us much about his life, but I really liked him. I wish I had known him while he was alive. I would've given him the nickname MI6."

Ashlyn's eyes widened. "The Secret Intelligence Service? Do you know how many times I mentioned that to him? Wow, now I really believe you." She stirred her latte as Tasha brought Chase's tea over. "Thank you, Brie. I know I haven't been the best person to you. But maybe we can start over."

"I'd like that," I said and gently grasped her extended hand. We had something in common. The boys we loved were gone and in heaven. I could help her through the coming days, months, or however long it took to be okay.

I stood and put on my coat. "Right now, I have to get to work. I'll call you later. Both of you."

I was elated to be back at the flower shop. I don't even know how the owners got on without me. The back room had no logic to it. Mrs. Glaston had totally undone all of my organization.

She came rushing at me with an armful of flowers. "Gabriella, I need you to deadhead the mums in back. To—"

"Extend the blooming period and maintain their beautiful appearance, right?" I grinned, leaning my elbows on the counter.

"You're absolutely right." She set the blooms on the counter. "Oh, and here is something I know will interest you as a future botanist."

Mrs. Glaston never tired of sharing facts about flowers and plants. Her loose gray bun was collapsing. She re-secured it as she spoke. "In 2017, Japanese scientists created the first true blue chrysanthemums through genetic engineering."

"That recent? I would've thought they'd been around for years before that."

"No, according to the Royal Horticultural Society's color scale, most of what we considered true blue was really violet or purple."

I nodded. "That's pretty cool info. Thanks."

"Oh, finish your social media photos first." She gestured to my phone on the counter. "The customers are loving your work. I actually have an online presence."

I held up my phone to snap a shot, and Mrs. Glaston covered her face with her hand. "Do you see how my bun is disrespecting me right now? Please don't take a picture of me."

I had taken over the photography and video footage for the flower shop's social media pages. They'd been horrible before. Mrs. Glaston didn't know anything about online stuff.

The doorbell chimed and customers walked in as I went to the back room. I walked to the green cabinet below the rolls of ribbon, and my phone vibrated. I pulled it out and looked at the screen.

Chase: I got those digits.

Me: 👀 Tasha?

Chase: I'm the man 🐻

Me: 🐱 Took you long enough. Gotta go.

A smile covered my face as I reached into the cabinet for the shears. Chase was putting himself out there. Good for him. Then I thought about how Micah used to joke that I worked at the '*Little Shop of Horrors.*' I'd had no idea what he was talking about, so he rented the movie, and we had watched it on his laptop.

Now, I sang the theme song in my head, danced around the room, and dropped the shears. They slid behind an old rusted white cabinet, which stood behind the green one. "Great, Brie. You know better. You don't dance with sharp objects."

Mrs. Glaston had a lot of stuff back there she said she was going to get rid of, so I had to push some boxes aside to reach the spot.

"She is going to kill me if I lose her favorite shears." I pulled the green cabinet out as far as I could and reached behind it. "Sheesh how far back did it slide?" I shined the flashlight from my phone under the cabinet. It picked up something tiny and brown.

"What is that? Is that a—"

I remembered the day I had let Micah do homework here in the back while I worked out front. Mrs. Glaston had been out that afternoon. I laughed to myself as I picked up the brown, dust-covered chocolate peanut.

"Always eating M&Ms."

There was enough room for me to squeeze in between the cabinets. I sat beside the white one and reached my hand back as far as I could for the shears. My fingers touched something that felt like nylon. I grabbed it and pulled, and then shined my phone back there again.

I froze for a moment, then pushed the cabinet away with my feet and pulled out the bag, which was identical to the one we found at the Bodega.

"Micah, what did you do?" I sat hugging the bag to my chest. A hard lump formed in my throat as I unzipped it and removed one of the green flower shop envelopes. Inside, I found a letter in Micah's handwriting:

Gabby, don't freak out. I knew you would find this. And I know you didn't expect the bag to be filled with floral foam blocks and this letter. If you're reading this without me ... I think you know the rest. Check your bank account, Gabby, and don't tell anyone about it. I know you're going to be a great botanist. Have a wonderful life, Gabby. I'm sorry for everything. I love you.

Micah.

P. S. Don't worry, I took care of my family too.

Tears flowed freely and dripped from my face onto the letter, causing the blue ink to run. I hadn't checked my bank account since Micah had gotten sick. For all I knew, it was overdrawn. Even in passing, Micah was still taking care of me.

When I finally stood, I removed the foam and stuffed the bag and letter into my backpack. From that point, my shift seemed to crawl by. Afterward, I went to the nearest coffee shop and purchased a chai latte. I sat at a table away from everyone else and logged into my bank account.

The numbers flashed on my phone screen. "Holy crap!" I inhaled sharply as my gaze landed on a balance far beyond what I could've imagined Micah had deposited.

I burst into loud sobs. I don't know if the people around me thought I was crazy or a sobbing mess, but I didn't care. Micah was the type of person who thought about other people more than he thought about himself. He was the type of person who would do anything for the people he loved. And he'd thought about me, knowing my dream was to go to college.

"I'm okay," I said to no one in particular. I stood, grabbed my backpack, and headed home.

That night, I lay in bed watching Elle sleep. We'd started reading together each night, and then she'd go back to her room. This week's book was *The Girl Who Looked Beyond the Stars.* We were two-thirds of the way through it. I closed the book and climbed out of bed.

I stood in my bathroom in the dark, and my hand inched toward the light switch. *Perhaps one more time?* I closed my eyes, took a deep breath, and switched on the light. I smiled at myself in the mirror. For a moment, I relived seeing Micah's reflection and handprint. That memory had replaced all thoughts of his funeral.

I examined my fuller face and unruly ponytail.

"I love you," I said.

And for the first time in my life, I was talking to me.

Please Leave A Review

I hope you enjoyed reading *Never Really Gone*. Your review means the world to me. I greatly appreciate any kind words. Even one or two sentences go a long way. The number of reviews a book receives greatly improves how well it does in bookstores. Even a short review would be wonderful. Thank you in advance.

Author Note

Want to be notified when my next book releases? Preorder pricing will always save you 40%! Subscribe on my website.

About the Author

L. B. Anne is best known for her Christian fiction, Sheena Meyer, book series about a girl with a special gift, and a destiny to save the world. L. B. Anne lives on the Gulf Coast of Florida with her husband and is a full-time author, speaker, and mental health advocate. When she's not inventing new obstacles for her diverse characters to overcome, you can find her reading, playing bass guitar, running on the beach, or downing a mocha iced coffee at a local cafe while dreaming of being your favorite author. Visit L. B. at www.lbanne.com

Facebook: facebook.com/authorlbanne
Instagram: Instagram.com/authorlbanne
Twitter: twitter.com/authorlbanne
Pinterest: pinterest.com/AuthorLBAnne